FIVE FALL INTO ADVENTURE

The FAMOUS FIVE *are*
Julian, Dick, George (Georgina by rights),
Anne, and Timothy the dog

Ragamuffin Jo could have been George's
double – it was astonishing how much alike
they were. And Jo had a way with dogs, too.
She was fearless, and could climb like a cat,
which was lucky when it came to making a
quick get-away from Red Tower.
The Five certainly met adventure when they
met Jo on Kirrin beach.

The ninth in the FAMOUS FIVE *series*

———

Ask your local bookseller, or at your
public library, for details of other
Knight Books, or write to the
Editor-in-Chief, Knight Books,
Arlen House, Salisbury Road,
Leicester LE1 7QS

Enid Blyton

Five fall into
adventure

Illustrated by Betty Maxey

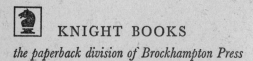

KNIGHT BOOKS

the paperback division of Brockhampton Press

ISBN 0 340 04141 2

This edition first published 1968 by Knight Books
the paperback division of Brockhampton Press Ltd, Leicester
Fifth impression 1970

Printed and bound in Great Britain by
Cox & Wyman Ltd, London, Reading and Fakenham

First published by Hodder & Stoughton Ltd 1950
Tenth impression 1965
Reissued by Brockhampton Press Ltd 1968
Illustrations copyright © 1968 Brockhampton Press Ltd

CONTENTS

FIVE FALL INTO ADVENTURE

Chapter One

AT KIRRIN COTTAGE AGAIN

GEORGINA was at the station to meet her three cousins. Timmy her dog was with her, his long tail wagging eagerly. He knew quite well they had come to meet Julian, Dick and Anne, and he was glad. It was much more fun when the Five were all together.

'Here comes the train, Timmy!' said George. Nobody

called her Georgina, because she wouldn't answer if they did. She looked like a boy with her short curly hair and her shorts and open-necked shirt. Her face was covered with freckles, and her legs and arms were as brown as a gipsy's.

There was the far-off rumble of a train, and as it came nearer, a short warning hoot. Timmy whined and wagged his tail. He didn't like trains, but he wanted this one to come.

Nearer and nearer it came, slowing down as it reached Kirrin station. Long before it came to the little platform three heads appeared out of one of the windows, and three hands waved wildly. George waved back, her face one big smile.

The door swung open almost before the train stopped. Out came a big boy, and helped down a small girl. Then came another boy, not quite so tall as the first one, with a bag in each hand. He dragged a third bag out, and then George and Timmy were on him.

'Julian! Dick! Anne! Your train's late; we thought you were never coming!'

'Hallo, George! Here we are at last. Get down, Timmy, don't eat me.'

'Hallo, George! Oh, Timmy, you darling – you're just as licky as ever!'

'Woof,' said Timmy joyfully, and bounded all round like a mad thing, getting into everybody's way.

'Any trunk or anything?' asked George. 'Only those three bags?'

'Well, we haven't come for long this time, worse luck,'

said Dick. 'Only a fortnight! Still, it's better than nothing.'

'You shouldn't have gone off to France all those six weeks,' said George, half-jealously. 'I suppose you've gone all French now.'

Dick laughed, waved his hands in the air and went off into a stream of quick French that sounded just like gibberish to George. French was not one of her strong subjects.

'Shut up,' she said, giving him a friendly shove. 'You're just the same old idiot. Oh, I'm so glad you've come. It's been lonely and dull at Kirrin without you.'

A porter came up with a barrow. Dick turned to him waved his hands again, and addressed the astonished man in fluent French. But the porter knew Dick quite well.

'Go on with you,' he said. 'Argy-bargying in double-Dutch like that. Do you want me to wheel these up to Kirrin Cottage for you?'

'Yes, please,' said Anne. 'Stop it, Dick. It isn't funny when you go on so long.'

'Oh, let him go on,' said George, and she linked her arms in Anne's and Dick's. 'It's lovely to have you again. Mother's looking forward to seeing you all.'

'I bet Uncle Quentin isn't,' said Julian, as they went along the little platform, Timmy capering round them.

'Father's in quite a good temper,' said George. 'You know he's been to America with Mother, lecturing and hearing other scientists lecturing too. Mother says everyone made a great fuss of him, and he liked it.'

George's father was a brilliant scientist, well-known all

over the world. But he was rather a difficult man at home, impatient, hot-tempered and forgetful. The children were fond of him, but held him in great respect. They all heaved a sigh of relief when he went away for a few days, for then they could make as much noise as they liked, tear up and down the stairs, play silly jokes and generally be as mad as they pleased.

'Will Uncle Quentin be at home all the time we're staying with you?' asked Anne. She was really rather afraid of her hot-tempered uncle.

'No,' said George. 'Mother and Father are going away for a tour in Spain – so we'll be on our own.'

'Wizard!' said Dick. 'We can wear our bathing costumes all day long then if we want to.'

'And Timmy can come in at meal-times without being sent out whenever he moves,' said George. 'He's been sent out every single meal-time this week, just because he snapped at the flies that came near him. Father goes absolutely mad if Timmy suddenly snaps at a fly.

'Shame!' said Anne, and patted Timmy's rough-haired back. 'You can snap at every single fly you like, Timmy, when we're on our own.'

'Woof,' said Timmy, gratefully.

'There won't be time for any adventure these hols,' said Dick, regretfully, as they walked down the lane to Kirrin Cottage. Red poppies danced along the way, and in the distance the sea shone as blue as cornflowers. 'Only two weeks – and back we go to school! Well, let's hope the weather keeps fine. I want to bathe six times a day!'

Soon they were all sitting round the tea-table at Kirrin Cottage, and their Aunt Fanny was handing round plates of her nicest scones and tea-cake. She was very pleased to see her nephews and niece again.

'Now George will be happy,' she said, smiling at the hungry four. 'She's been going about like a bear with a sore head the last week or two. Have another scone, Dick? Take two while you're about it.'

'Good idea,' said Dick, and helped himself. 'Nobody makes scones and cakes like you do, Aunt Fanny. Where's Uncle Quentin?'

'In his study,' said his aunt. 'He knows it's tea-time, and he's heard the bell, but I expect he's buried in something or other. I'll have to fetch him in a minute. I honestly believe he'd go without food all day long if I didn't go and drag him into the dining-room!'

'Here he is,' said Julian, hearing the familiar impatient footsteps coming down the hall to the dining-room. The door was flung open. Uncle Quentin stood there, a newspaper in his hand, scowling. He didn't appear to see the children at all.

'Look here, Fanny!' he shouted. 'See what they've put in this paper – the very thing I gave orders was NOT to be put in! The dolts! The idiots! The . . .'

'Quentin! Whatever's the matter?' said his wife. 'Look – here are the children – they've just arrived.'

But Uncle Quentin simply didn't see any of the four children at all. He went on glaring at the paper. He rapped at it with his hand.

'*Now* we'll get the place full of reporters wanting to see

me, and wanting to know all about my new ideas!' he said, beginning to shout. 'See what they've said! "This eminent scientist conducts all his experiments and works out all his ideas at his home, Kirrin Cottage. Here are his stack of notebooks, to which are now added two more – fruits of his visit to America, and here at his cottage are his amazing diagrams," and so on and so on.'

'I tell you, Fanny, we'll have hordes of reporters down.'

'No, we shan't, dear,' said his wife. 'And, anyway, we are soon off to Spain. Do sit down and have some tea. And look, can't you say a word to welcome Julian, Dick and Anne?'

Uncle Quentin grunted and sat down. 'I didn't know they were coming,' he said, and helped himself to a scone. 'You might have told me, Fanny.'

'I told you three times yesterday and twice today,' said his wife.

Anne suddenly squeezed her uncle's arm. She was sitting next to him. 'You're just the same as ever, Uncle Quentin,' she said. 'You never, never remember we're coming! Shall we go away again?'

Her uncle looked down at her and smiled. His temper never lasted very long. He grinned at Julian and Dick. 'Well, here you are again!' he said. 'Do you think you can hold the fort for me while I'm away with your aunt?'

'Rather!' said all three together.

'We'll keep everyone at bay!' said Julian. 'With Timmy's help. I'll put up a notice: *"Beware, very fierce dog"*.'

'Woof,' said Timmy, sounding delighted. He thumped

his tail on the floor. A fly came by his nose and he snapped at it. Uncle Quentin frowned.

'Have another scone, Father?' said George hurriedly. 'When are you and Mother going to Spain?'

'Tomorrow,' said her mother firmly. 'Now don't look like that, Quentin. You know perfectly well it's been arranged for weeks, and you *need* a holiday, and if we don't go tomorrow all our arrangements will be upset.'

'Well, you might have *warned* me it was tomorrow,' said her husband, looking indignant. 'I mean – I've all my notebooks to check and put away, and . . .'

'Quentin, I've told you heaps of times that we leave on September the third,' said his wife, still more firmly. '*I* want a holiday, too. The four children will be quite all right here with Timmy – they'll love being on their own. Julian is almost grown-up now and he can cope with anything that turns up.'

Timmy snapped twice at a fly, and Uncle Quentin jumped. 'If that dog does that again,' he began, but his wife interrupted him at once.

'There, you see! You're as touchy and nervy as can be, Quentin, dear. It will do you good to get away – and the children will have a lovely two weeks on their own. Nothing can possibly happen, so make up your mind to leave tomorrow with an easy mind!'

Nothing can possibly happen? Aunt Fanny was wrong of course. *Anything* could happen when the Five were left on their own!

Chapter Two

A MEETING ON THE BEACH

It really was very difficult to get Uncle Quentin off the next day. He was shut up in his study until the last possible moment, sorting out his precious notebooks. The taxi arrived and hooted outside the gate. Aunt Fanny, who had been ready for a long time, went and rapped at the study door.

'Quentin! Unlock the door! You really must come. We shall lose the plane if we don't go now.'

'Just one minute!' shouted back her husband. Aunt Fanny looked at the four children in despair.

'That's the fourth time he's called out "Just one minute",' said George. The telephone shrilled out just then, and she picked up the receiver.

'Yes,' she said. 'No, I'm afraid you can't see him. He's off to Spain, and nobody will know where he is for the next two weeks. What's that? Wait a minute – I'll ask my mother.'

'Who is it?' said her mother.

'It's the *Daily Clarion*,' said George. 'They want to send a reporter down to interview Daddy. I told them he was going to Spain – and they said could they publish that?'

'Of course,' said her mother, thankfully, 'Once that's in the papers nobody will ring up and worry you. Say, yes, George.'

George said yes, the taxi hooted more loudly than ever, and Timmy barked madly at the hooting. The study door was flung open and Uncle Quentin stood in the doorway, looking as black as thunder.

'Why can't I have a little peace and quiet when I'm doing important work?' he began. But his wife made a dart at him and dragged him down the hall. She put his hat in one hand, and would have put his stick into the other if he hadn't been carrying a heavy despatch case.

'You're not doing important work, you're off on a holiday,' she said. 'Oh, Quentin, you're worse than ever! What's that case in your hand? Surely you are not taking work away with you?'

The taxi hooted again, and Timmy woofed just behind Uncle Quentin. He jumped violently, and the telephone rang loudly.

'That's another reporter coming down to see you, Father,' said George. 'Better go quickly!'

Whether that bit of news really did make Uncle Quentin decide at last to go, nobody knew — but in two seconds he was sitting in the taxi, still clutching his despatch case, telling the taxi-driver exactly what he thought of people who kept hooting their horns.

'Good-bye, dears,' called Aunt Fanny, thankfully. 'Don't get into mischief. We're off at last.'

The taxi disappeared down the lane. 'Poor Mother!' said George. 'It's always like this when they go for a holiday. Well, there's one thing certain – I shall NEVER marry a scientist.'

Everyone heaved a sigh of relief at the thought that Uncle Quentin was gone. When he was over-worked he really was impossible.

'Still, you simply have to make excuses for anyone with a brain like his,' said Julian. 'Whenever our science master at school speaks of him, he almost holds his breath with awe. Worst of it is, he expects *me* to be brilliant because I've got a brilliant uncle.'

'Yes. It's difficult to live up to clever relations,' said Dick. 'Well – we're on our own, except for Joan. Good old Joan! I bet she'll give us some smashing meals.'

'Let's go and see if she's got anything we can have now,' said George. 'I'm hungry.'

'So am I,' said Dick. They marched down the hall into the kitchen, calling for Joan.

'Now, you don't need to tell me what you've come for,' said Joan, the smiling, good-tempered cook. 'And I don't need to tell you this – the larder's locked.'

'Oh Joan – what a mean thing to do!' said Dick.

'Mean or not, it's the only thing to do when all four of you are around, to say nothing of that great hungry dog,' said Joan, rolling out some pastry vigorously. 'Why, last holidays I left a meat pie and half a tongue and a cherry tart and trifle sitting on the shelves for the next day's meals – and when I came back from my half-day's outing there wasn't a thing to be seen.'

'Well, we thought you'd left them there for our supper,' said Julian, sounding quite hurt.

'All right – but you won't get the chance of thinking anything like that again,' said Joan, firmly. 'That larder door's going to be kept locked. Maybe I'll unlock it sometimes and hand you out a snack or two – but I'm the one that's going to unlock it, not you.'

The four drifted out of the kitchen again, disappointed. Timmy followed at their heels. 'Let's go down and have a bathe,' said Dick. 'If I'm going to have six bathes a day, I'd better hurry up and have my first one.'

'I'll get some ripe plums,' said Anne. 'We can take those down with us. And I expect the ice-cream man will come along to the beach too. We shan't starve! And we'd better wear our shirts and shorts over our bathing costumes, so we don't catch too much sun.'

Soon they were all down on the sand. They found a good place and scraped out comfortable holes to sit in. Timmy scraped his own.

'I can't imagine why Timmy bothers to scrape one,' said George. 'Because he always squeezes into mine sooner or later. Don't you, Timmy?'

Timmy wagged his tail, and scraped so violently that they were all covered with sand. 'Pooh!' said Anne, spitting sand out of her mouth. 'Stop it, Timmy. As fast as I scrape my hole, you fill it up!'

Timmy paused to give her a lick, and then scraped again, making a very deep hole indeed. He lay down in it, panting, his mouth looking as if he were smiling.

'He's smiling again,' said Anne. 'I never knew a dog that smiled like Timmy. Timmy, it's nice to have you again.'

'Woof,' said Timmy, politely, meaning that it was nice to have Anne and the others back again, too. He wagged his tail and sent a shower of sand over Dick.

They all wriggled down comfortably into their soft warm holes. 'We'll eat the plums first and then we'll have a bathe,' said Dick. 'Chuck me one, Anne.'

Two people came slowly along the beach. Dick looked at them out of half-closed eyes. A boy and a man – and what a ragamuffin the boy looked! He wore torn dirty shorts and a filthy jersey. No shoes at all.

The man looked even worse. He slouched as he came, and dragged one foot. He had a straggly moustache and mean, clever little eyes that raked the beach up and down. The two were walking at high-water mark and were obviously looking for anything that might have been cast up by the tide. The boy already had an old box, one wet shoe and some wood under his arm.

'What a pair!' said Dick to Julian. 'I hope they don't come near us. I feel as if I can smell them from here.'

The two walked along the beach and then back. Then, to the children's horror, they made a bee-line for where they were lying in their sandy holes, and sat down close beside them. Timmy growled.

An unpleasant, unwashed kind of smell at once came to the children's noses. Pooh! Timmy growled again. The boy took no notice of Timmy's growling. But the man looked uneasy.

'Come on – let's have a bathe,' said Julian, annoyed at the way the two had sat down so close to them. After all, there was practically the whole of the beach to choose from – why come and sit almost on top of somebody else?

When they came back from their bathe the man had gone, but the boy was still there – and he had actually sat himself down in George's hole.

'Get out,' said George, shortly, her temper rising at once. 'That's my hole, and you jolly well know it.'

'Findings keepings,' said the boy, in a curious sing-song voice. 'It's my hole now.'

George bent down and pulled the boy roughly out of the hole. He was up in a trice, his fists clenched. George clenched hers, too.

Dick came up at a run. 'Now, George – if there's any fighting to be done, I'll do it,' he said. He turned to the scowling boy. 'Clear off! We don't want you here!'

The boy hit out with his right fist and caught Dick unexpectedly on the jawbone. Dick looked astounded. He hit out, too, and sent the tousle-headed boy flying.

'Yah, coward!' said the boy, holding his chin tenderly. 'Hitting someone smaller than yourself! I'll fight that first boy, but I won't fight *you*.'

'You can't fight him,' said Dick. 'He's a girl. You can't fight girls – and girls oughtn't to fight, anyway.'

'Ses you!' said the dirty little ragamuffin, standing up and doubling his fists again. 'Well, you look here – *I'm* a girl, too – so I can fight her all right, can't I?'

George and the ragamuffin stood scowling at one another, each with fists clenched. They looked so astonishingly alike, with their short, curly hair, brown freckled faces and fierce expressions that Julian suddenly roared with laughter. He pushed them firmly apart.

'Fighting forbidden!' he said. He turned to the raga-muffin. 'Clear off!' he ordered. 'Do you hear me? Go on – off with you!'

The gipsy-like girl stared at him. Then she suddenly burst into tears and ran off howling.

'*She's* a girl all right,' said Dick, grinning at the howls. 'She's got some spunk though, facing up to me like that. Well, that's the last we'll see of *her*!'

But he was wrong. It wasn't!

Chapter Three

FACE AT THE WINDOW

THE five curled up in their holes once more. Dick felt his jaw-bone. 'That ragamuffin of a girl gave me a good bang,' he said, half-admiringly. 'Little demon, isn't she! A bit of live wire!'

'I can't see why Julian wouldn't let me have a go at her,' said George sulkily. 'It was my hole she sat in – she *meant* to be annoying! How dare she?'

'Girls can't go about fighting,' said Dick. 'Don't be an ass, George. I know you make out you're as good as a boy, and you dress like a boy and climb trees as well as I can – but it's really time you gave up thinking you're as good as a boy.'

This sort of speech didn't please George at all. 'Well, anyway, I don't burst into howls if I'm beaten,' she said, turning her back on Dick.

'No, you don't,' agreed Dick. 'You've got as much spunk as any boy – much more than that other kid had. I'm sorry I sent her flying now. It's the first time I've ever hit a girl, and I hope it'll be the last.'

'I'm jolly glad you hit her,' said George. 'She's a nasty little beast. If I see her again I'll tell her what I think of her.'

'No, you won't,' said Dick. 'Not if I'm there, anyway. She had her punishment when I sent her flying.'

'Do shut up arguing, you two,' said Anne, and sent a shower of sand over them. 'George, don't go into one of your moods, for goodness' sake – we don't want to waste a single day of this two weeks.'

'Here's the ice-cream man,' said Julian, sitting up and feeling for the waterproof pocket in the belt of his bathing trunks. 'Let's have one each.'

'Woof,' said Timmy, and thumped his tail on the sand.

'Yes, all right – one for you, too,' said Dick. 'Though what sense there is in giving *you* one, I don't know. One lick, one swallow, and it's gone. It might be a fly for all you taste of it.'

Timmy gulped his ice-cream down at once and then went into George's hole, squeezing beside her, hoping for a lick of her ice, too. But she pushed him away.

'No, Timmy. Ice-cream's wasted on you! You can't even have a lick of mine. And do get back into your hole – you're making me frightfully hot.'

Timmy obligingly got out and went into Anne's hole. She gave him a little bit of her ice-cream. He sat panting beside her, looking longingly at the rest of the ice. 'You're melting it with your hot breath,' said Anne. 'Go into Julian's hole now!'

The five of them had a thoroughly lazy morning. As none of them had a watch they went in far too early for lunch, and were shooed out again by Joan.

'How you can come in at ten past twelve for a one o'clock lunch, I don't know!' she scolded. 'I haven't even finished the housework yet.'

'Well – it *felt* like one o'clock,' said Anne, disappointed to find there was so long to wait. Still, when lunch-time came, Joan really did them well.

'Cold ham and tongue – cold baked beans – beetroot – crisp lettuce straight from the garden – heaps of tomatoes – cucumber – hard-boiled egg!' recited Anne in glee.

'Just the kind of meal I like,' said Dick, sitting down. 'What's for pudding?'

'There it is on the sideboard,' said Anne. 'Wobbly blancmange, fresh fruit salad and jelly. I'm glad I'm hungry.'

'Now don't you give Timmy any of that ham and tongue,' Joan warned George. 'I've got a fine bone for him. Coming, Timmy?'

Timmy knew the word 'bone' very well indeed. He trotted after Joan at once, his feet sounding loudly in the hall. They heard Joan talking kindly to him in the kitchen as she found him his bone.

'Good old Joan,' said Dick. 'She's like Timmy – her bark is worse than her bite.'

'Timmy's got a good bite, though,' said George, helping herself to three tomatoes at once. 'And his bite came in useful heaps of times for us.'

They ate steadily, thinking of some of the hair-raising adventures they had had, when Timmy and his bite had certainly come in very useful. Timmy came in after a while, licking his lips.

'Nothing doing, old chap,' said Dick, looking at the empty dishes on the table. 'Don't tell me you've chomped up that bone already!'

Timmy had. He lay down under the table, and put his nose on his paws. He was happy. He had had a good meal, and he was with the people he loved best. He put his head as near George's feet as he could.

'Your whiskers are tickling me,' she said, and screwed up her bare toes. 'Pass the tomatoes, someone.'

'You *can't* manage any more tomatoes, surely!' said Anne. 'You've had five already.'

'They're out of my own garden,' said George, 'so I can eat as many as I like.'

After lunch they lazed on the beach till it was time for a bathe again. It was a happy day for all of them – warm, lazy, with plenty of fun and romping about.

George looked out for the ragamuffin girl, but she didn't appear again. George was half sorry. She would have liked a battle of words with her, even if she couldn't have a fight!

They were all very tired when they went to bed that night. Julian yawned so loudly when Joan came in with a jug of hot cocoa and some biscuits that she offered to lock up the house for him.

'Oh, no, thank you, Joan,' said Julian at once. 'That's the man's job, you know, locking up the house. You can trust me all right. I'll see to every window and every door.'

'Right, Master Julian,' said Joan, and bustled away

to wind up the kitchen clock, rake out the fire, and go up to bed. The children went up, too, Timmy, as usual, at George's heels. Julian was left downstairs to lock up.

He was a very responsible boy. Joan knew that he wouldn't leave a single window unfastened. She heard him trying to shut the little window in the pantry, and she called down:

'Master Julian! It's swollen or something, and won't shut properly. You needn't bother about it, it's too small for anyone to get into !'

'Right !' said Julian, thankfully, and went upstairs. He yawned a terrific yawn again, and set Dick off, too, as soon as he came into the bedroom they both shared. The girls, undressing in the next room, laughed to hear them.

'*You* wouldn't hear a burglar in the middle of the night, Julian and Dick !' called Anne. 'You'll sleep like logs !'

'Old Timmy can listen out for burglars,' said Julian, cleaning his teeth vigorously. 'That's his job, not mine. Isn't it, Timmy ?'

'Woof,' said Timmy, clambering on to George's bed. He always slept curled up in the crook of her knees. Her mother had given up trying to insist that George didn't have Timmy on her bed at night. As George said, even if *she* agreed to that, Timmy wouldn't !

Nobody stayed awake for more than five seconds. Nobody even said anything in bed, except for a sleepy good night. Timmy gave a little grunt and settled down, too, his head on George's feet. It was heavy, but she liked it there. She put out a hand and stroked Timmy gently.

He licked one of her feet through the bed-clothes. He loved George more than anyone in the world.

It was dark outside that night. Thick clouds had come up and put out all the stars. There was no sound to be heard but the wind in the trees and the distant surge of the sea – and both sounded so much the same that it was hard to tell the difference.

Not another sound – not even an owl hooting to its mate, or the sound of a hedgehog pattering in the ditch.

Then why did Timmy wake up? Why did he open first one eye and then another? Why did he prick up his ears and lie there, listening? He didn't even lift his head at first. He simply lay listening in the darkness.

He lifted his head cautiously at last. He slid off the bed as quietly as a cat. He padded across the room and out of the door. Down the stairs he went, and into the hall, where his claws rattled on the tiled floor. But nobody heard him. Everyone in the house was fast asleep.

Timmy stood and listened in the hall. He knew he had heard something. Could it have been a rat somewhere? Timmy lifted his nose and sniffed.

And then he stiffened from head to tail, and stood as if turned into stone. Something was climbing up the wall of the house. Scrape, scrape, scrape – rustle, rustle! Would a rat dare to do that?

Upstairs, in her bed, Anne didn't know why she suddenly woke up just then, but she did. She was thirsty, and she thought she would get a drink of water. She felt for her torch, and switched it on.

The light fell on the window first, and Anne saw something that gave her a terrible shock. She screamed loudly, and dropped her torch in fright. George woke up at once. Timmy came bounding up the stairs.

'Julian! wailed Anne. 'Come quickly. I saw a face at the window, a horrible, dreadful face looking in at me!'

George rushed to the window, switching on her torch as she did so. There was nothing there. Timmy went with her. He sniffed at the open window and growled.

'Hark – I can hear someone running quickly down the path,' said Julian, who now appeared with Dick. 'Come on, Timmy – downstairs with you and after them!'

And down they all went – Anne too. They flung the front door wide and Timmy sped out, barking loudly. A face at the window? He'd soon find out who it belonged to!

Chapter Four

THE NEXT DAY

THE four children waited at the open front door, listening to Timmy's angry, excited barking. Anne was trembling, and Julian put his arm round her comfortingly.

'What was this dreadful face like?' he asked her. Anne shivered in his arm.

'I didn't see very much,' she said. 'You see, I just switched on my torch, and the beam was directed on the window nearby – and it lighted up the face for a second. It had nasty gleaming eyes, and it looked very dark – perhaps it was a black man's face! Oh, I *was* frightened!'

'Then did it disappear?' asked Julian.

'I don't know,' said Anne. 'I was so frightened that I dropped my torch and the light went out. Then George woke up and rushed to the window.'

'Where on earth was Timmy?' said Dick, feeling suddenly surprised that Timmy hadn't awakened them all by barking. Surely he must have heard the owner of the face climbing up to the window?

'I don't know. He came rushing into the bedroom when I screamed,' said Anne. 'Perhaps he *had* heard a noise and had gone down to see what it was.'

'That's about it,' said Julian. 'Never mind, Anne. It

was a tramp, I expect. He found all the doors and windows downstairs fastened – and shinned up the ivy to see if he could enter by way of a bedroom. Timmy will get him, that's certain.'

But Timmy didn't get him. He came back after a time, with his tail down, and a puzzled look in his eyes. 'Couldn't you find him, Timmy?' asked George, anxiously.

'Woof,' said Timmy, mournfully, his tail still down. George felt him. He was wet through.

'Goodness! Where have you been to get so wet?' she said, in surprise. 'Feel him, Dick.'

Dick felt him, and so did the others. 'He's been in the sea,' said Julian. 'That's why he's wet. I guess the burglar, or whatever he was, must have sprinted down to the beach, when he knew Timmy was after him – and jumped into a boat! It was his only chance of getting away.'

'And Timmy must have swum after him till he couldn't keep up any more,' said George. 'Poor old Tim. So you lost him, did you?'

Timmy wagged his tail a little. He looked very down-hearted indeed. To think he had heard noises and thought it was a rat – and now, whoever it was had got away from him. Timmy felt ashamed.

Julian shut and bolted the front door. He put up the chain, too. 'I don't think the Face will come back again in a hurry,' he said. 'Now he knows there's a big dog here he'll keep away. I don't think we need worry any more.'

They all went back to bed again. Julian didn't go to

sleep for some time. Although he had told the others not to worry, he felt worried himself. He was sorry that Anne had been frightened, and somehow the boldness of the burglar in climbing up to a bedroom worried him, too. He must have been determined to get in somehow.

Joan, the cook, slept through all the disturbance. Julian wouldn't wake her. 'No,' he said, 'don't tell her anything about it. She'd want to send telegrams to Uncle Quentin or something.'

So Joan knew nothing about the night's happenings, and they heard her cheerfully humming in the kitchen the next morning as she cooked bacon and eggs and tomatoes for their breakfast.

Anne was rather ashamed of herself when she woke up and remembered the fuss she had made. The Face was rather dim in her memory now. She half wondered if she had dreamed it all. She asked Julian if he thought she might have had a bad dream.

'Quite likely,' said Julian, cheerfully, very glad that Anne should think this. 'More than likely! I wouldn't worry about it any more, if I were you.'

He didn't tell Anne that he had examined the thickly-growing ivy outside the window, and had found clear traces of the night-climber. Part of the sturdy clinging ivy-stem had come away from the wall, and beneath the window were strewn broken-off ivy leaves. Julian showed them to Dick.

'There *was* somebody,' he said. 'What a nerve he had, climbing right up to the window like that. A real cat-burglar! '

'What was that?' said George indignantly. 'Did you throw something at me, Dick?'

'No,' said Dick, his eyes glued to his book.

Something else hit George on the back of the neck, and she put her hand up with an exclamation. 'What's happening? Who's throwing things?'

She looked to see what had hit her. Lying on the sand was a small roundish thing. George picked it up. 'Why – it's a damson stone,' she said. And 'Ping'! Another one hit her on the shoulder. She leapt up in a rage.

She could see nobody at all. She waited for another damson stone to appear, but none did.

'I just wish I could draw your face, George,' said Julian,

with a grin. 'I never saw such a frown in my life. Ooch!'

The 'ooch!' was nothing to do with George's frown; it was caused by another damson stone that caught Julian neatly behind the ear. He leapt to his feet too. A helpless giggle came from behind a rock some way behind and above them. George was up on the ledge in a second.

Behind one of the rocks sat the ragamuffin girl. Her pockets were full of damsons, some of them spilling out as she rolled on the rocks, laughing. She sat up when she saw George, and grinned.

'What do you mean, throwing those stones at us?' demanded George.

'I wasn't throwing them,' said the girl.

'Don't tell lies,' said George scornfully. 'You know you were.'

'I wasn't. I was just spitting them,' said the awful girl. 'Watch!' She slipped a stone into her mouth, took a deep breath and then spat out the stone. It flew straight at George and hit her sharply and squarely on the nose. George looked so extremely surprised that Dick and Julian roared with laughter.

'Bet I can spit stones farther than any of you,' said the ragamuffin. 'Have some of my damsons and see.'

'Right!' said Dick promptly. 'If you win I'll buy you an ice-cream. If I do, you can clear off from here and not bother us any more. See?'

'Yes,' said the girl, and her eyes gleamed and danced. 'But I shall win!'

Chapter Five

RAGAMUFFIN JO

GEORGE was most astonished at Dick. How very shocking to see who could spit damson stones out the farthest.

'It's all right,' said Julian to her in a low voice. 'You know how good Dick is at that sort of game. He'll win – and we'll send the girl scooting off, well and truly beaten.'

'I think you're horrible, Dick,' said George, in a loud voice. 'Horrible!'

'Who used to spit cherry-stones out and try and beat me last year?' said Dick at once. 'Don't be so high-and-mighty, George.'

Anne came slowly back from her pool, wondering why the others were up on the rocks. Damson stones began to rain round her. She stopped in astonishment. Surely – surely it couldn't be the others doing that? A stone hit her on her bare arm, and she squealed.

The ragamuffin girl won handsomely. She managed to get her stones at least three feet farther than Dick. She lay back, laughing, her teeth gleaming very white indeed.

'You owe me an ice-cream,' she said, in her sing-song voice. Julian wondered if she was Welsh. Dick looked at her, marvelling that she managed to get her stones so far.

'I'll buy you the ice-cream, don't worry,' he said. 'Nobody's ever beaten me before like that, not even Stevens, a boy at school with a most enormous mouth.'

'I do think you really are dreadful,' said Anne. 'Go and buy her the ice-cream and tell her to go home.'

'I'm going to eat it here,' said the girl, and she suddenly looked exactly as mulish and obstinate as George did when she wanted something she didn't think she would get.

'You look like George now!' said Dick, and immediately wished he hadn't. George glared at him, furious.

'What! That nasty, rude tangly-haired girl like *me*!' stormed George. 'Pooh! I can't bear to go near her.'

'Shut up,' said Dick, shortly. The girl looked surprised.

'What does she mean?' she asked Dick. 'Am I nasty? You're as *rude* as I am, anyway.'

'There's an ice-cream man,' said Julian, afraid that the hot-tempered George would fly at the girl and slap her. He whistled to the man, who came to the edge of the rocks and handed out six ice-creams.

'Here you are,' said Julian, handing one to the girl. 'You eat that up and go.'

They all sat and ate ice-creams, George still scowling. Timmy gulped his at once as usual. 'Look – he's had all his,' marvelled the girl. 'I call that a waste. Here, boy – have a bit of mine!'

To George's annoyance, Timmy licked up the bit of ice-cream thrown to him by the girl. How *could* Timmy accept anything from her?

Dick couldn't help being amused by this queer, bold

little girl, with her tangled short hair and sharp darting eyes. He suddenly saw something that made him feel uncomfortable.

On her chin the girl had a big black bruise. 'I say,' said Dick, '*I* didn't give you that bruise yesterday, did I?'

'What bruise? Oh, this one on my chin?' said the girl, touching it. 'Yes, that's where you hit me when you sent me flying. *I* don't mind. I've had plenty worse ones from my Dad.'

'I'm sorry I hit you,' said Dick, awkwardly. 'I honestly thought you were a boy. What's your name?'

'Jo,' said the girl.

'But that's a *boy's* name,' said Dick.

'So's George. But you said she was a girl,' said Jo, licking the last bits of ice-cream from her fingers.

'Yes, but George is short for Georgina,' said Anne. 'What's Jo short for?'

'Don't know,' said Jo. 'I never heard. All I know is I'm a girl and my name is Jo.'

'It's probably short for Josephine,' said Julian. They all stared at the possible Josephine. The short name of Jo certainly suited her – but not the long and pretty name of Josephine.

'It's really queer,' said Anne, at last, 'but Jo *is* awfully like you, George – same short curly hair – only Jo's is terribly messy and tangly – same freckles, dozens of them – same turned-up nose . . .'

'Same way of sticking her chin up in the air, same scowl, same glare!' said Dick. George put on her fiercest glare at these remarks, which she didn't like at all.

'Well, all I can say I hope I haven't her layers of dirt and her sm –' she began, angrily. But Dick stopped her.

'She's probably not got any soap or hair-brush or anything. She'd be all right cleaned up. Don't be unkind, George.'

George turned her back. How *could* Dick stick up for that awful girl? 'Isn't she ever going?' she said. 'Or is she going to park herself on us all day long?'

'I'll go when I want to,' said Jo, and put on a scowl, so exactly like George's that Julian and Dick laughed in surprise. Jo laughed, too, but George clenched her fists furiously. Anne looked on in distress. She wished Jo would go, then everything would be all right again.

'I like that dog,' said Jo, suddenly, and she leaned over to where Timmy lay beside George. She patted him with a hand that was like a little brown paw. George swung round.

'Don't touch my dog!' she said. '*He* doesn't like you, either!'

'Oh, but he does,' said Jo, surprisingly. 'All dogs like *me*. So do cats. I can make your dog come to me as easy as anything.'

'Try!' said George, scornfully. 'He won't go to *you*! Will you, Tim?'

Jo didn't move. She began to make a queer little whining noise down in her throat, like a forlorn puppy. Timmy pricked up his ears at once. He looked inquiringly at Jo. Jo stopped making the noise and held out her hand.

Timmy looked at it and turned away – but when he heard the whining again he got up, listening. He stared intently at Jo. Was this a kind of dog-girl, that she could so well speak his language?

Jo flung herself on her face and went on with the small, whining noises that sounded as if she were a small dog in pain or sorrow. Timmy walked over to her and sat down, his head on one side, puzzled. Then he suddenly bent down and licked the girl's half-hidden face. She sat up at once and put her arms round Timmy's neck.

'Come here, Timmy,' said George, jealously. Timmy shook off the brown arms that held him and walked over to George at once.

Jo laughed.

'See? I made him come to me and give me one of his best licks! I can do that to any dog.'

'How can you?' asked Dick, in wonder. He had never seen Timmy make friends before with anyone who was disliked by George.

'I don't know, really,' said Jo, pushing back her hair again, as she sat up. 'I reckon it's in the family. My mother was in a circus, and she trained dogs for the ring. We had dozens – lovely they were. I loved them all.'

'Where is your mother?' asked Julian. 'Is she still in the circus?'

'No. She died,' said Jo. 'And I left the circus with my Dad. We've got a caravan. Dad was an acrobat till he hurt his foot.'

The four children remembered how the man had dragged his foot as he walked. They looked silently at dirty little Jo. What a strange life she must have led!

'She's dirty, she's probably very good at telling lies and

thieving, but she's got pluck,' thought Julian. 'Still, I'll be glad when she goes.'

'I wish I hadn't given her that awful bruise,' thought Dick. 'I wonder what she'd be like cleaned up and brushed? She looks as if a little kindness would do her good.'

'I'm sorry for her, but I don't much like her,' thought Anne.

'I don't believe a word she says!' thought George angrily. 'Not one word! She's a humbug. And I'm *ashamed* of Timmy for going to her. I feel very cross with him.'

'Where's your father?' asked Julian at last.

'Gone off somewhere to meet somebody,' said Jo vaguely. 'I'm glad. He was in one of his tempers this morning. I went and hid under the caravan.'

There was a silence. 'Can I stay with you today till

my Dad comes back?' said Jo suddenly, in her sing-song voice. 'I'll wash myself if you like. I'm all alone today.'

'No. We don't want you,' said George, feeling as if she really couldn't bear Jo any longer. 'Do we, Anne?'

Anne didn't like hurting anyone. She hesitated. 'Well,' she said at last, 'perhaps Jo *had* better go.'

'Yes,' said Julian. 'It's time you scooted off now, Jo. You've had a long time with us.'

Jo looked at Dick with mournful eyes, and touched the bruise on her chin as if it hurt her. Dick felt most uncomfortable again. He looked round at the others.

'Don't you think she could stay and share our picnic?' he said. 'After all — she can't *help* being dirty and — and ...'

'It's all right,' said Jo, suddenly scrambling up. 'I'm going! There's my Dad!'

They saw the man in the distance, dragging his foot as he walked. He caught sight of Jo and gave a shrill and piercing whistle. Jo made a face at them all, an impudent, ugly, insolent face.

'I don't like you!' she said. Then she pointed at Dick. 'I only like *him* — he's nice. Yah to the rest of you!'

And off she went like a hare over the sand, her bare feet hardly touching the ground.

'What an extraordinary girl!' said Julian. 'I don't feel we've seen the last of her yet!'

Chapter Six

WHAT HAPPENED IN THE NIGHT?

THAT night Anne began to look rather scared as darkness fell. She was remembering the Face at the Window!

'It won't come again, Ju, will it?' she said to her big brother half a dozen times.

'No, Anne. But if you like I'll come and lie down on George's bed instead of George tonight, and stay with you all night long,' said Julian.

Anne considered this and then shook her head. 'No. I think I'd almost rather have George and Timmy. I mean – George and I – and even you – might be scared of Faces, but Timmy wouldn't. He'd simply leap at them.'

'You're quite right,' said Julian. 'He would. All right then, I won't keep you company – but you'll see, nothing whatever will happen tonight. Anyway, if you like, we'll all close our bedroom windows and fasten them, even if we are too hot for anything – then we'll know nobody can possibily get in.'

So that night Julian not only closed all the doors and windows downstairs as he had done the night before

44

(except the tiny pantry window that wouldn't shut), but he also shut and fastened all the ones upstairs.

'What about Joan's window?' asked Anne.

'She *always* sleeps with it shut, summer and winter,' said Julian, with a grin. 'Country folk often do. They think the night air's dangerous. Now you've nothing at all to worry about, silly.'

So Anne went to bed with her mind at rest. George drew the curtains across their window so that even if the Face came again they wouldn't be able to see it!

'Let Timmy out for me, Julian, will you?' called George. 'Anne doesn't want me to leave her, even to take old Timmy out for his last walk. Just open the door and let him out. He'll come in when he's ready.'

'Right!' called Julian, and opened the front door. Timmy trotted out, tail wagging. He loved his last sniff round. He liked to smell the trail of the hedgehog who was out on his night-rounds; he liked to put his nose down a rabbit-hole and listen to stirrings down below; and he loved to follow the meanderings of rats and mice round by the thick hedges.

'Isn't Timmy in yet?' called George from the top of the stairs. 'Do call him, Ju. I want to get into bed. Anne's half-asleep already.'

'He'll be in in a moment,' said Julian, who wanted to finish his book. 'Don't fuss.'

But no Timmy had appeared even when he had finished his book. Julian went to the door and whistled. He listened for Timmy to come. Then, hearing nothing, he whistled once more.

This time he heard the sound of pattering footsteps coming up the path to the door. 'Oh there you are, Tim,' said Julian. 'What have you been up to? Chasing rabbits or something?'

Timothy wagged his tail feebly. He didn't jump up at Julian as he usually did. 'You look as if you've been up to some mischief, Tim,' said Julian. 'Go on – up to bed with you – and mind you bark if you hear the smallest sound in the night.'

'Woof,' said Timmy, in rather a subdued voice, and went upstairs. He climbed on to George's bed and sighed heavily.

'What a sigh!' said George. 'And what have you been eating, Timmy? Pooh – you've dug up some frightful old bone, I know you have. I've a good mind to push you off my bed. I suppose you suddenly remembered one you buried months ago. Pooh!'

Timmy wouldn't be pushed off the bed. He settled down to sleep, his nose on George's feet as usual. He snored a little, and woke George in about half an hour.

'Shut up, Timmy,' she said, pushing him with her feet. Anne woke up, alarmed.

'What is it, George?' she whispered, her heart thumping.

'Nothing. Only Timmy snoring. Hark at him. He won't stop,' said George, irritated. 'Wake up, Timmy, and stop snoring.'

Timmy moved sleepily and settled down again. He stopped snoring and George and Anne fell sound asleep. Julian woke once, thinking he heard something fall – but hearing Timmy gently snoring again through the open doors of the two rooms, he lay down, his mind at rest.

If the noise had *really* been a noise Timmy would have heard it, no doubt about that. George always said that Timmy slept with one ear open.

Julian heard nothing more till Joan went downstairs at seven o'clock. He heard her go into the kitchen and do something to the kitchen grate. He turned over and fell asleep again.

He was wakened suddenly twenty minutes later by loud screams from downstairs. He sat up and then leapt out of bed at once. He rushed downstairs. Dick followed him.

'Look at this! The master's study – turned upside down – those drawers ransacked! The safe's open, too. Mercy me, who's been here in the night – with all the doors locked and bolted, too!' Joan wailed loudly and wrung her hands as she gazed at the untidy room.

'I say!' said Dick, horrified. 'Someone's been search-ing for something pretty thoroughly! Even got the safe open – and wrenched the drawers out.'

'How did he get in?' said Julian, feeling bewildered. He went round the house, looking at doors and windows. Except for the kitchen door, which Joan said she had unlocked and unbolted herself as soon as she came down, not a window or door had been touched. All were fastened securely.

Anne came down, looking scared. 'What's the matter?' she said. But Julian brushed her aside. How did that burglar get in? That was what he wanted to know. Through one of the *upstairs* windows, he supposed – one

T—c

that somebody had opened last night after he had fastened
it. Perhaps in the girls' room?

But no – not one window was open. All were fastened
securely, including Joan's. Then a thought struck him
as he looked into George's room. Why hadn't Timmy
barked? After all, there must have been quite a bit of
noise, however quiet the thief had been. He had himself
heard something and had awakened. Why hadn't Timmy,
then?

George was trying to pull Timmy off the bed. 'Ju, Ju!
There's something wrong with Timmy. He won't wake
up!' she cried. 'He's breathing so heavily, too – just listen
to him! And what's the matter downstairs? What's
happened?'

Julian told her shortly while he examined Timmy.
'Somebody got in last night – your father's study's in
the most awful mess – absolutely ransacked from top to
bottom, safe and all. Goodness knows how the fellow got
in to do it.'

'How awful!' said George, looking very pale. 'And
now something's wrong with Tim. He didn't wake up
last night when the burglar came – he's ill, Julian!'

'No, he's not. He's been doped,' said Julian, pulling
back Timmy's eyelids. 'So *that's* why he was so long outside last night! Somebody gave him some meat or something with dope in – some kind of drug. And he ate it,
and slept so soundly that he never heard a thing – and
isn't even awake yet.'

'Oh, Julian – will he be all right?' asked George
anxiously, stroking Timmy's motionless body. 'But how

could he take any food from a stranger in the night?'

'Maybe he picked it up – the burglar may have flung it down hoping that Timmy would eat it,' said Julian. 'Now I understand why he looked so sheepish when he came in. He didn't even jump up and lick me.'

'Oh, dear – Timmy, do, do wake up,' begged poor George, and she shook the big dog gently. He groaned a little and snuggled down again.

'Leave him,' said Julian. 'He'll be all right. He's not poisoned, only drugged. Come down and see the damage !'

George was horrified at the state of her father's study. 'They were after his two special books of American notes, I'm sure they were,' she said. 'Father said that any other country in the world would be glad to have those. Whatever are we to do?'

'Better get in the police,' said Julian, gravely. 'We can't manage this sort of thing ourselves. And do you know your father's address in Spain?'

'No,' wailed George. 'He and Mother said they were going to have a *real* holiday this time – no letters to be forwarded, and no address left till they had been settled somewhere for a few days. Then they'd telegraph it.'

'Well, we'll certainly have to get the police in, then,' said Julian, looking rather white and stern. George glanced at him. He seemed suddenly very grown-up indeed. She watched him go out of the room. He went into the hall and rang up the police station. Joan was very relieved.

'Yes, get in the police, that's what we ought to do,' she said. 'There's that nice Constable Wilkins, and that other one with the red face, what's he called – Mr. Donaldson. I'll be making some coffee for them when they come.'

She cheered up considerably at the thought of handing out cups of her good hot coffee to two interested policemen, who would ask her plenty of questions that she would be only too delighted to answer. She bustled off to the kitchen.

The four children stared silently at the ruins of the study. What a mess! Could it ever be cleared up? Nobody would know what was gone till Uncle Quentin came back. How furious he would be.

'I hope nothing very important has been taken,' said Dick. 'It looks as if somebody knew there was something valuable here, and meant to get it!'

'And has probably got it,' said Julian. 'Hallo – that must be the police! Come on – I can see it will be a long time before we get our breakfast this morning!'

Chapter Seven

POLICEMEN IN THE HOUSE

THE police were very, very thorough. The children got tired of them long before lunch-time. Joan didn't. She made them cups of coffee and put some of her home-made buns on a plate and sent Anne to pick up ripe plums. She felt proud to think that it was she who had discovered the ransacked study.

There were two policemen. One was a sergeant, rather solemn and very correct. He interviewed each of the children and asked them exactly the same questions. The other man went over the study bit by bit, very thoroughly indeed.

'Looking for finger-prints, I suppose,' said Anne. 'Oh dear – when can we go and bathe?'

The thing that puzzled everyone, the police included, was – how did the thief or thieves get in? Both policemen went round the house, slowly and deliberately trying every door and window still locked or fastened. They stood and looked at the pantry window for some time.

'Got in there, I suppose,' said one of them.

'Must have been as small as a monkey then,' said the other. He turned to Anne, who was the smallest of the four children. 'Could you squeeze through there, Missy, do you think?'

'No,' said Anne. 'But I'll try if you like.' So she tried – but she stuck fast before she got even half-way through, and Julian had to pull hard to get her down again.

'Have you any idea what has been stolen, sir?' the sergeant asked Julian, who seemed extraordinarily grown-up that morning.

'No, sergeant – none of us has,' said Julian. 'Not even George here, who knows her father's work better than any of us. The only thing we know is that my uncle went to America to lecture a short time ago – and he brought back two notebooks, full of valuable diagrams and notes. He did say that other countries might be very glad to get hold of those. I expect they were in that safe.'

'Well – they'll certainly be gone then,' said the sergeant, shutting his own fat notebook with a snap. 'Pity when people leave such things in an ordinary safe – and then go off without leaving an address. Can't we possibly get in touch with him? This may be terribly important.'

'I know,' said Julian, looking worried. 'We shall have an address in a day or two – but I honestly don't see how we can get in touch before then.'

'Right,' said the sergeant. 'Well – we'll go now – but we'll bring back a photographer with us after lunch to photograph the room – then your cook can tidy it up. I know she's longing to.'

'Coming back *again*!' said Anne, when the two men had solemnly walked down the path, mounted very solid-looking bicycles, and gone sailing down the lane. 'Good gracious! Have we got to answer questions all over again?'

'Well, we'll go down to the beach and take a boat and go rowing,' said Julian, with a laugh. 'We'll be out of reach then. I don't see that we can give them any more help. I must say it's all very peculiar – I wish to goodness I knew how the thief got in.'

George had been very quiet and subdued all the morning. She had worried about Timmy, fearing that he had been poisoned, and not merely drugged, as Julian had said. But Timmy was now quite recovered, except that he seemed a bit sleepy still, and not inclined to gambol round in his usual ridiculous way. He looked extremely sheepish, too.

'I can't think why Timmy looks like that,' said George, puzzled. 'He usually only puts that look on when he's done something he's ashamed of – or got into mischief. He couldn't possibly know, could he, that whatever he picked up and ate last night was something he shouldn't eat?'

'No,' said Dick. 'He's sensible though, I think, not to touch poisoned meat – but he couldn't know if some harmless sleeping powder had been put into anything. It might have no smell and no taste. Perhaps he's just ashamed of being so sleepy!'

'If only he'd been awake!' groaned George. 'He would have heard any noise downstairs at once – and he'd have barked and waked us all, and flown downstairs himself to attack whoever was there! Why, oh why didn't

I take him out myself last night as I usually do?'

'It was a chapter of accidents,' said Julian. 'You didn't take him out, so he was alone – and it happened that someone was waiting there with drugged food – which he either found or took from the thief. . . .'

'*No*,' said George. 'Timmy would never, never take anything from someone he didn't know. I've always taught him that.'

'Well, he got it somehow – and slept through the very night he should have been awake,' said Julian. 'What I'm so afraid of, George, is that the thieves have got your father's two American notebooks. They seem to have left most of the stuff – piles and piles of books of all kinds, filled with your father's tiny handwriting.'

Joan came in to say lunch was ready. She told the children that the policemen had eaten every one of her home-made buns. She still felt important and excited, and was longing to get out to the village and tell everyone the news.

'You'd better stay in and give the policemen a good tea,' said Julian. 'They're coming back with a photographer.'

'Then I'd better do another baking,' said Joan, pleased.

'Yes. Make one of your chocolate cakes,' said Anne.

'Oh, do you think they'd like one?' said Joan.

'Not for *them*, Joan – for us, of course!' said George. 'Don't waste one of your marvellous chocolate cakes on policemen. Can you make us up a picnic tea? We're fed up with being indoors – we're going out in a boat.'

Joan packed them a good tea after they had had their

lunch and they all set off before the police came back.
Timmy was much less sleepy now and did a little caper
round them as they walked to the beach. George brightened up at once.

'He's getting better,' she said. 'Timmy, I simply shan't
let you out of my sight now! If anyone's going to dope
you again they'll have to do it under my very nose.'

They had a lovely time out in George's boat. They
went half-way to Kirrin Island and bathed from the boat,
diving in and having swimming races till they were tired
out. Timmy joined them, though he couldn't swim nearly
as fast as they could.

'He doesn't really *swim*,' said Anne. 'He just tries to
run through the water. I wish he'd let me ride on his
back like a sea-dog – but he always slips away under me
when I try.'

'They got back about six o'clock to find that the policemen had eaten the whole of the chocolate cake that Joan
had made, besides an extraordinary amount of scones and
buns.

Also the study was now tidied up, and a man had come
to mend the safe. Everything was safely back there, though
the police had told Joan that if there was anything of
real value it should be handed to them till George's father
came back.

'But we don't know which of all those papers are valuable!' said Julian. 'Well – we'll have to wait till Uncle
Quentin cables us – and that may not be for days.
Anyway, I don't expect we'll be worried by the thief
again – he's got what he wanted.'

The exciting happenings of the day had made them all tired except Julian. 'I'm off to bed,' said Dick, about nine o'clock. 'Anne, why don't you go? You look fagged out.'

'Yes, I will,' said Anne. 'Coming, George?'

'I'm going to take Timmy out for his last walk,' said George. 'I shall never let him go out alone at night again. Come on, Timmy. If you want to go to bed I'll lock up the front door, Ju.'

'Right,' said Julian. 'I'll go up in a minute. I don't fancy staying down here by myself tonight. I'll fasten everything and lock up, except the front door. Don't forget to put up the chain, too, George – though I'm pretty certain we don't need to expect any more burglaries!'

'Or faces at the window,' said Anne, at once.

'No,' said Julian. 'There won't be any more of those either. Good night, Anne – sleep well!'

Anne and Dick went upstairs. Julian finished the paper he was reading, and then got up to go round the house and lock up. Joan was already upstairs, dreaming of policemen eating her chocolate cakes.

George went out with Timmy. He ran eagerly to the gate and then set off down the lane for his usual night walk with George. At a gate in the lane he suddenly stood still and growled as if he saw something unusual.

'Silly, Timmy!' said George, coming up. 'It's only somebody camping in a caravan! Haven't you seen a caravan before! Stop growling!'

They went on, Timmy sniffing into every rathole and rabbit-hole, enjoying himself thoroughly. George was enjoying the walk, too. She didn't hurry – Julian could always go up to bed if he didn't want to wait.

Julian did go up to bed. He left the front door ajar, and went yawning upstairs, suddenly feeling sleepy. He got into bed quietly and quickly seeing that Dick was already asleep. He lay awake listening for George. When he was half asleep, he heard the front door shut.

'There she is,' he thought, and turned over to go to sleep.

But it wasn't George. Her bed was empty all that night, and nobody knew, not even Anne. George and Timmy didn't come back!

Chapter Eight

WHERE CAN GEORGE BE?

ANNE woke up in the night, feeling thirsty. She whispered across the room:

'George! Are you awake?'

There was no answer, so, very cautiously and quietly Anne got herself a drink from the decanter on the washstand. George was sometimes cross if she was awakened in the middle of the night. Anne got back into bed, not guessing that George hadn't answered because she wasn't there!

She fell asleep and didn't wake till she heard Dick's voice. 'Hey, you two – get up; it's a quarter to eight. We're going for a bathe!'

Anne sat up, yawning. Her eyes went to George's bed. It was empty. More than that, it was all neat and tidy, as if it had just been made!

'*Well!*' said Anne in astonishment. 'George is up already, and has even made her bed. She *might* have waked me, and I could have gone out with her. It's such a lovely day. I suppose she's taken Timmy for an early morning walk, like she sometimes does.'

Anne slipped into her bathing costume and ran to join the boys. They went downstairs together, their bare feet padding on the carpet.

'George has gone out already,' said Anne. 'I expect she woke early and took Timmy; I never even heard her!'

Julian was now at the front door. 'Yes,' he said. 'The door isn't locked or bolted – George must have slipped down, undone it and then just pulled the door softly to. How very considerate of her! Last time she went out early she banged the door so hard that she woke everyone in the house!'

'She may have gone fishing in her boat,' said Dick. 'She said yesterday she'd like to some early morning when the tide was right. She'll probably arrive complete with stacks of fish for Joan to cook.'

They looked out to sea when they got to the beach. There was a boat far out on the water with what looked like two people in it, fishing.

'I bet that's George and Timmy,' said Dick. He yelled and waved his hands, but the boat was too far away, and nobody waved back. The three of them plunged into the cold waves. Brrrr-rrr-rrr!

'Lovely!' said Anne, when they came out again, the drops of sea-water running down their bodies and glistening in the early morning sun. 'Let's have a run now.'

They chased one another up and down the beach, and then, glowing and very hungry, went back to breakfast.

'Where's George?' asked Joan, as she brought in their breakfast. 'I see her bed's made and all – what's come over her?'

'I think she's out fishing with Timmy,' said Dick. 'She was up and about long before we were.'

'I never heard her go,' said Joan. 'She must have been very quiet. There you are now – there's a fine breakfast for you – sausages and tomatoes and fried eggs!'

'O-o-o-o-h, lovely,' said Anne. 'And you've done the sausages just how I like them, Joan – all bursting their skins. Do you think we'd better eat George's too? She's still out in the boat. She may not be back for ages.'

'Well, then you'd better eat her share,' said Joan. 'I've no doubt she took something out of the larder before she went. Pity I didn't lock it last night, as usual!'

They finished George's share between them and then started on toast and marmalade. After that Anne went to help Joan make the beds and dust and mop. Julian and Dick went off to the village to do the morning's shopping at the grocer's.

Nobody worried about George at all. Julian and Dick came back from their shopping and saw the little boat still out on the sea.

'George will be absolutely starving by the time she comes back,' said Julian. 'Perhaps she's got one of her moods on and wants to be alone. She was awfully upset about Timmy being drugged.'

They met the ragamuffin Jo. She was walking along the beach, collecting wood, and she looked sullen and dirtier than ever.

'Hallo, Jo!' called Dick. She looked up and came towards them without a smile. She looked as if she had been crying. Her small brown face was streaked where the tears had run through the dirt.

'Hallo!' she said, looking at Dick. She looked so miser-

able that Dick felt touched.

'What's the matter, kid?' he said, kindly.

Tears trickled down Jo's face as she heard the kindness in his voice. She rubbed them away and smudged her face more than ever.

'Nothing,' she said. 'Where's Anne?'

'Anne's at home, and George is out in that boat with Timmy fishing,' said Dick, pointing out to sea.

'Oh!' said Jo, and turned away to go on with her collecting of wood. Dick went after her.

'Hey!' he said. 'Don't go off like that. You just tell me what's wrong with you this morning.'

He caught hold of Jo and swung her round to face him.

He looked closely at her and saw that she now had two bruises on her face – one going yellow, that he had given her when he had sent her flying two or three days before – and a new one, dark purple.

'Where did you get *that* bruise?' he said, touching it lightly.

'That was my dad,' said Jo. 'He's gone off and left me – taken the caravan and all! I wanted to go, too; but he wouldn't let me into the caravan. And when I hammered at the door, he came out and pushed me down the steps. That's when I got this bruise – and I've got another on my leg, too.'

Dick and Julian listened in horror. What kind of a life was this that Jo had to live? The boys sat down on the beach, and Dick pulled Jo down between them.

'But surely your father is coming back?' said Julian. 'Is the caravan your only home?'

'Yes,' said Jo. 'I've never had another home. We've always lived in a caravan. Mum did, too, when she was alive. Things were better then. But this is the first time Dad's gone off without me.'

'But – how are you going to live?' asked Dick.

'Dad said Jake would give me money to buy food,' said Jo. 'But only if I do what he tells me. I don't like Jake. He's mean.'

'Who's Jake?' asked Julian, most astonished at all this.

'Jake's a gipsy fellow. He knows my father,' said Jo. 'He's always turning up for a day or two, and going away again. If I wait about here, he'll come and give me a sixpence or two, I expect.'

'What will he tell you to do?' said Dick, puzzled. 'It all seems very queer and horrible to me. You're only a kid.'

'Oh, he may tell me to go poaching with him or – or – well, there's things we do that folks like you don't,' said Jo, suddenly realizing that Dick and Julian would not at all approve of some of the things she did. 'I hope he gives me some money today, though. I haven't got any at all, and I'm hungry.'

Dick and Julian looked at one another. To think that in these days there should be a forlorn waif like Jo, going in fear of others, and often hungry and lonely.

Dick put his hand in the shopping basket and pulled out a packet of chocolate and some biscuits. 'Here you are,' he said. 'Tuck into these – and if you'd like to go to the kitchen door some time today and ask Joan, our cook, for a meal, she'll give you one. I'll tell her about you.'

'Folks don't like me at kitchen doors,' said Jo, cramming biscuits into her mouth. 'They're afraid I'll steal something.' She glanced up at Dick. 'And I do,' she said.

'You shouldn't do that,' said Dick.

'Well, wouldn't you, if you were so hungry you couldn't even bear to look at a baker's cart?' said Jo.

'No – I don't think so. At least, I hope not,' said Dick, wondering what he really would feel like if he were starving. 'Where's this Jake fellow?'

'I don't know. Somewhere about,' said Jo. 'He'll find me when he wants me. I've got to stay on the beach, Dad said. So I couldn't come to your house, anyway. I dursent leave here.'

The boys got up to go, worried about this little raga-muffin. But what could they do? Nothing, except feed her and give her money. Dick had slipped a shilling into her hand, and she had pocketed it without a word, her eyes gleaming.

George was still not home by lunch-time; and now Julian for the first time began to feel anxious. He slipped out to the beach to see if the boat was still at sea. It was just pulling in – and with a sinking heart Julian saw that it was not George and Timmy who were in it, but two boys.

He went to look for George's boat – and there it was, high up on the boat-beach with many others. George had not been out in it at all!

He ran back to Kirrin Cottage and told the others. They were at once as anxious as he was. What *could* have become of George?

'We'll wait till tea-time,' said Julian. 'Then if she's not back we'll really have to do something about it – tell the police, I should think. But she *has* sometimes gone off for the day before, so we'll just wait a bit longer.'

Tea-time came – but no George, and no Timmy. Then they heard someone pattering up the garden path – was it Timmy? They leaned out of the window to see.

'It's Jo,' said Dick, in disappointment, 'She's got a note or something. Whatever does *she* want?'

Chapter Nine

AN EXTRAORDINARY MESSAGE –
AND A PLAN

JULIAN opened the front door. Jo silently gave him a plain
envelope. Julian tore it open, not knowing what in the
least to expect. Jo turned to go – but Julian put out his
hand and caught hold of her firmly, whilst he read the
note in complete amazement.

'Dick!' he called. 'Hold on to Jo. Don't let her go.
Better take her indoors. This is serious.'

Jo wasn't going to be taken indoors. She squealed, and wriggled like an eel. Then she began to kick Dick viciously with her bare feet.

'Let me go! I'm not doing any harm. I only brought you that note!'

'Stop squealing and being silly,' said Dick. 'I don't want to hurt you, you know that. But you must come indoors.'

But Jo wouldn't stop wriggling and pulling and kicking. She looked scared out of her life. It was as much as Dick and Julian could do to get the little wriggler into the dining-room and shut the door. Anne followed, looking very frightened. Whatever was happening?

'Listen to this,' said Julian, when the door was shut. 'It's unbelievable!' He held out the typewritten note for the others to see as he read it out loud.

'We want the second notebook, the one with figures in, and we mean to have it. Find it and put it under the last stone on the crazy paving path at the bottom of the garden. Put it there tonight.

'We have got the girl and the dog. We will set them free when we have what we want from you. If you tell the police, neither the girl nor the dog will come back. The house will be watched to see that nobody leaves it to warn the police. The telephone wires are cut.

'When it is dark, put the lights on in the front room and all three of you sit there with the maid Joan, so that we can keep a watch on you. Let the big boy leave the house at eleven o'clock, shining a torch and put the notebook where we said. He must then go back to the lighted

room. You will hear a hoot like an owl when we have collected it. The girl and the dog will then be returned.'

This amazing and terrifying note made Anne burst into tears and cling to Julian's arm.

'Julian! Julian! George can't have come back from her walk with Timmy last night! She must have been caught then – and Timmy, too. Oh, why didn't we start hunting for her then?'

Julian looked very grim and white. He was thinking hard. 'Yes – someone was lying in wait, I've no doubt – and she and Timmy were kidnapped. Then the kidnapper – or one of them – came back to the house and shut the front door to make it seem as if George was back. And someone has probably been hanging round all day to find out whether we're worried about George, or just think she's gone off for the day!'

'Who gave you the note?' said Dick, sharply, to the scared Jo.

She trembled.

'A man,' she said.

'What sort of a man?' asked Julian.

'I don't know,' said Jo.

'Yes, you do,' said Dick. 'You *must* tell, Jo.'

Jo looked sullen. Dick shook her, and she tried to get away. But he held her far too tightly. 'Go on – tell us what the fellow was like,' he said.

'He was tall and had a long beard and a long nose and brown eyes,' rattled off Jo suddenly. 'And he was dressed in fisherman's clothes, and – he spoke foreign.'

The two boys looked sternly at her. 'I believe you're making all that up, Jo,' said Julian.

'I'm not,' said Jo sulkily. 'I'd never seen him before, so there.'

'Jo,' said Anne, taking Jo's brown little paw in hers, 'tell us truly anything you know. We're so very worried about George.' Tears sprang out of her eyes as she spoke, and she gave a little wail.

'Serve that George-girl right if she's got taken away,' said Jo fiercely. 'She was rude to me – she's crool and unkind. Serve her right, I say. I wouldn't tell you anything – not even if I knew something to tell.'

'You *do* know something,' said Dick. 'You're a bad little girl, Jo. I shan't have anything more to do with you. I felt sorry and unhappy about you, but now I don't.'

Jo looked sullen again, but her eyes were bright with tears. She turned away. 'Let me go,' she said. 'I tell you, that fellow gave me half-a-crown to bring this note to you, and that's all I know. And I'm *glad* George is in trouble. People like her deserve it, see!'

'Let her go,' said Julian wearily. 'She's like a savage little cat – all claws and spite. I thought there might be some good in her, but there isn't.'

'I thought so, too,' said Dick, letting go Jo's arm. 'I quite liked her. Well, go, Jo. We don't want you any more.'

Jo rushed to the door, wrenched it open, and fled down the hall and out of the house. There was a silence after she had gone.

'Julian,' whispered Anne. 'What are we going to do?'

Julian said nothing. He got up and went into the hall. He picked up the telephone receiver and put his ear to it, listening for the faint crackling that would tell him he was connected to the exchange. After a moment he put it back again.

'No connection,' he said. 'The wires have been cut, as the note said. And no doubt there's somebody on watch to see we don't slip out to give warning. This is all crazy. It can't be true.'

'But it is,' said Dick. 'Horribly true. Julian, do you know what notebook they want? I've no idea!'

'Nor have I,' said Julian. 'And it's impossible to go and hunt for it, because the safe has been mended and locked – and the police have the key.'

'Well, that's that, then,' said Dick. 'What are we going to do? Shall I slip out and warn the police?'

Julian considered. 'No,' he said at last. 'I think these people mean business. It would be terrible if anything happened to George. Also, you might be caught and spirited away yourself. There are people watching the house, don't forget.'

'But Julian – we can't just sit here and do nothing!' said Dick.

'I know. This will have to be thought about carefully,' said Julian. 'If only we knew where George had been taken to! We could rescue her then. But I can't see how we can find out.'

'If one of us went and hid down the bottom of the garden and waited to see whoever came to take up the notebook – we could follow the fellow and maybe he'd lead us to where George is hidden,' suggested Dick.

'You forget that we've all got to sit in the lighted front room, so it would easily be spotted if one of us were missing,' said Julian. 'Even Joan has to sit there. This is all very stupid and melodramatic.'

'Does anyone come to the house this evening? Any of the tradesmen, for instance?' asked Anne, again in a whisper. She felt as if people must be all round the house, listening and watching!

'No. Else we could give them a note,' said Julian. Then he gave the table a rap that made the others jump. 'Wait a bit! Yes, of course – the paper-boy comes! Ours is almost the last house he delivers at. But perhaps it would be risky to give him a note. Can't we think of something better?'

'Listen,' said Dick, his eyes shining. 'I've got it! I know the paper-boy. He's all right. We'll have the front door open and yank him in as soon as he appears. And I'll go out immediately, with his cap on, and his satchel of papers, whistling – jump on his bike and ride away. And none of the watchers will know I'm not the boy! I'll come back when it's dark, sneak round the garden at the bottom and hide to watch who comes for the hidden notebook – and I'll follow him!'

'Good idea, Dick!' said Julian, turning it quickly over in his mind. 'Yes – it's possible. It would be better to watch and see who comes rather than tell the police – because if these kidnappers mean business, George would certainly be in trouble once they knew we'd been able to get in touch with the police.'

'Won't the newspaper boy think it's queer?' asked Anne.

'Not very. He's a bit simple,' said Dick. 'He believes anything he's told. We'll make up something to satisfy him and give him such a good time that he'll want to keep visiting us!'

'About this notebook,' said Julian. 'We'd better get some kind of book out of one of the drawers and wrap it up with a note inside to say we hope it's the one. The fellow who comes to collect it will have to have some kind of parcel to take off with him to give to the kidnappers. It isn't likely he'd undo it and look at it – or even know if it was the right one or not.'

'Go and hunt out a book, Anne,' said Dick. 'I'll be looking out for the newspaper boy. He's not due till half-past seven, but I don't dare to risk missing him – and he may be early, you never know.'

Anne shot off to the study, thankful to have something to do. Her hands were trembling as she pulled out drawer after drawer to look for a big notebook that would do to wrap up in a parcel.

Julian went with Dick to the front door, to help him to deal with the unsuspecting newspaper boy. They stood there, patiently waiting, hearing the clock strike six o'clock, then half-past, then seven.

'Here he comes!' said Dick, suddenly. 'Now – get ready to yank him in! Hallo, Sid!'

Chapter Ten

SID'S WONDERFUL EVENING

SID, the paper-boy, was most amazed to find himself yanked quickly through the front door by Julian. He was even more amazed to find his very lurid check cap snatched off his head, and his bag of papers torn from his shoulder.

' 'Ere!' he said feebly. 'What you doing?'

'It's all right, Sid,' said Julian, holding him firmly. 'Just a joke. We've got a little treat in store for you.'

Sid didn't like jokes of this sort. He struggled, but soon gave it up. Julian was big and strong and very determined. Sid turned and watched Dick stride out with his bright check cap sideways on his head, and his paper-bag over his shoulder. He gasped when he saw Dick leap on the bicycle that he, Sid, had left by the gate, and go sailing off up the lane on it.

'What's he doing?' he asked Julian, amazed. 'Funny sort of joke this.'

'I know. Hope you don't mind,' said Julian, leading him firmly into the sitting-room.

'Somebody betted him he wouldn't deliver the papers, maybe?' said Sid. 'So he's taken the bet on?'

'You're clever, you are, Sid,' said Julian, and Sid

beamed all over his round, simple face.

'Well, I hope he'll deliver them all right,' he said. 'Anyway, there's only two more, up at the farm. Yours is the last house but one that I go to. When's he coming back?'

'Soon,' said Julian. 'Will you stay and have supper with us, Sid?'

Sid's eyes nearly fell out of his head. 'Supper with you folks?' he said. 'Coo! That'd be a rare treat!'

'All right. You sit and look at these books,' said Julian, giving him two or three story books belonging to Anne. 'I'll just go and tell our cook to make a specially nice supper for you.'

Sid was all at sea about this unexpected treat, but quite willing to accept a free meal and sit down. He sat beaming on the couch, turning over the pages of a fairy-story book. Coo! What would his mother say when she heard he'd had supper at Kirrin Cottage? She wouldn't half be surprised, thought Sid.

And now Julian had to tackle Joan, and get her to join in their little plot. He went into the kitchen and shut the door. He looked so grave that Joan was startled.

'What's the matter?' she said.

Julian told her. He told her about the kidnapping of George, and the strange note. He gave it to her to read. She sat down, her knees beginning to shake.

'It's the kind of thing you read in the papers, Master Julian,' she said, in rather a shaky voice. 'But it's queer when it happens to *you*! I don't like it – that's flat, I don't.'

'Nor do we,' said Julian, and went on to tell Joan all they had arranged to do. She smiled a watery smile when he told her how Dick had gone off as the paper-boy in order to watch who took the notebook that night, and described how surprised Sid was.

'That Sid!' she said. 'We'll never hear the last of it, down in the village – him being invited here to supper. He's simple, that boy, but there's no harm in him.

'I'll get him a fine supper, don't you worry. And I'll come and sit with you tonight in the lighted room – we'll play a card game, see? One that Sid knows – he's never got much beyond Snap and Happy Families.'

'That's a very good idea,' said Julian, who had been wondering how in the world they could amuse Sid all the evening. 'We'll play Snap – and let him win!'

Sid was quite overcome at his wonderful evening. First there was what he called a 'smasher of a supper,' with ham and eggs and chip potatoes followed by jam tarts and a big chocolate mould, of which Sid ate about three-quarters.

'I'm partial to chocolate mould,' he explained to Anne. 'Joan knows that – she knows I'm partial to anything in the chocolate line. She's friendly with my Mum, so she knows. The things I'm partial to I like very much, see?'

Anne giggled and agreed. She was enjoying Sid, although she was very worried and anxious. But Sid was so comical. He didn't mean to be. He was just enjoying himself hugely, and he said so every other minute.

In fact, he was really a very nice guest to have. It wasn't everybody who could welcome everything with so much gusto and say how wonderful it was half a dozen times on end.

He went out to the kitchen after supper and offered to wash up for Joan. 'I always do it for Mum,' he said. 'I won't break a thing.' So he did the washing up and Anne did the drying. Julian thought it was a good thing to give her as much to do as possible, to stop her worrying.

Sid looked a bit taken-aback when he was asked to play games later on. 'Well – I dunno,' he said. 'I'm not much good at games. I did try to learn draughts, but all that jumping over one another got me muddled. If I want to jump over things I'll play leap-frog and do the thing properly.'

'Well – we did think of playing Snap,' said Julian, and Sid brightened up at once.

'Snap! That's right up my street!' he said. And so it was. His habit of shouting snap and collecting all the cards at the same moment as his shout, led to his winning quite a lot of games. He was delighted.

'This is a smasher of an evening,' he kept saying. 'Don't know when I've enjoyed myself so much. Wonder how that brother of yours is getting on – hope he brings my bike back all right.'

'Oh, he will,' said Julian, dealing out the cards for the sixth game of Snap. They were all in the lighted sitting-room now, sitting round a table in the window – Julian, Joan, Anne and Sid. Anyone watching would see them clearly – and would certainly not guess that Sid, the fourth one, was the paper-boy and not Dick.

At eleven o'clock Julian left to put the parcel that Anne

had carefully wrapped up under the stone at the bottom of the garden. She had found a big notebook she thought would do, one that didn't seem at all important, and had wrapped it in paper and tied it with string. Julian had slipped a note inside.

Here is the notebook. Please release our cousin at once. You will get into serious trouble if you hold her any longer.

He slipped down the garden and shone his torch on the crazy paving there. When he came to the last stone he found that it had been loosened. He lifted it up easily and put the parcel into a hollow that seemed to have been prepared ready for it. He took a cautious look round, wondering if Dick was hidden anywhere about, but could see no one.

He was back in the lighted sitting-room in under two minutes, yelling 'Snap' with the others. He played stupidly, partly because he wanted the delighted Sid to win and partly because he was wondering about Dick. Was he all right?

An outbreak of owls hooting loudly made them all jump. Julian glanced at Joan and Anne, and they nodded. They guessed that it was the signal to tell them that the parcel had been found and collected. Now they could get rid of Sid, and wait for Dick.

Joan disappeared and came back with cups of chocolate and some buns. Sid's eyes gleamed. Talk about an evening!

Another hour was spent in eating and drinking and hearing Sid relate details of all the most exciting games of Snap he had ever played. He then went on to talk of Happy Families and seemed inclined to stay a bit longer and have a game at that.

'Your Mum will be getting worried about you,' said Julian, looking at the clock. 'It's very late.'

'Where's my bike?' said Sid, realizing with sorrow that his 'smasher of an evening' was now over. 'Hasn't that brother of yours come back yet? Well, you tell him to leave it at my house in time for my paper-round tomorrow morning. And my cap, too. That's my Special Cap, that is. I'm very partial to that cap – it's a bit of a smasher.'

'It certainly is,' agreed Julian, who was now feeling very tired. 'Now listen, Sid. It's very late, and there may be bad folks about. If anyone speaks to you, run for your life, and don't stop till you get home.'

'Coo,' said Sid, his eyes nearly falling out of his head. 'Yes, I'll run all right.'

He shook hands solemnly with each of them and departed. He whistled loudly to keep his spirits up. The village policeman came unexpectedly round a corner on rubber soles and made him jump.

'Now then, young Sid,' said the policeman, sternly. 'What you doing out this time of night?'

Sid didn't wait to answer. He fled and when he got home there was his bicycle by the front gate, complete with checked cap and paper-bag. 'That was a bit of all right!' thought Sid.

He glanced in disappointment at the dark windows of his house. Mum was in bed and asleep. Now he would have to wait till morning to tell her of his most remarkable evening.

And now, what had happened to Dick? He had shot out of the house and sailed away on Sid's bicycle, with Sid's dazzling cap on his head. He thought he saw a movement in the hedge nearby and guessed someone was hidden there, watching. He deliberately slowed down, got off his bicycle and pretended to do something to the wheel. Let the watcher see his bag of papers and be deceived into thinking he was without any doubt the paper-boy.

He rode to the farm and delivered the two papers there, then down to the village where he left Sid's things outside his house. Then he went into the cinema for a long while – until it was dark and he could safely creep back to Kirrin Cottage.

He set off at last, going a very roundabout way indeed. He came to the back of Kirrin garden. Where should he hide? Was anyone already hidden there? If so, the game was up – and he'd be caught, too!

Chapter Eleven

DICK MAKES A CAPTURE

Dick stood and listened, holding his breath. He could hear no sound except for the rustling of the trees around, and the sudden squeak of a field-mouse. It was a dark night and cloudy. Was there anyone hidden nearby, or could he find a hiding-place in safety and wait?

He thought for a few minutes, and decided that there wouldn't be anyone watching the back of the house now that it was dark. Julian and the others would be in full view of any watcher at the front, seated as they were in the lighted sitting-room — there would be no need for anyone to watch the back.

He debated where to hide and then made a quick decision. 'I'll climb a tree,' he thought. 'What about that one just near the crazy paving path? If the clouds clear away I could perhaps catch a glimpse of what the man's like who comes to collect the parcel. Then I'll shin quietly down the tree and stalk him.'

He climbed up into an oak tree that spread its broad branches over the path. He wriggled down in a comfortable fork and set himself to wait patiently.

What time had that note said? Eleven o'clock. Yes —

Julian was to go down at eleven o'clock and put the parcel under the stone. He listened for the church clock to strike. If the wind was in the right direction he would hear it clearly.

It struck just then. Half-past ten. Half an hour to wait. The waiting was the worst part. Dick put his hand into his pocket and brought out a bar of half-melted chocolate. He began to nibble it very gently, to make it last a long time.

The church clock struck a quarter to eleven. Dick finished the chocolate, and wondered if Julian would soon be along. Just as the clock began to chime the hour at eleven, the kitchen door opened and Dick saw Julian outlined in the opening. He had the parcel under his arm.

He saw Julian go swiftly down the path and sensed him looking all about. He dared not give the slightest hint to him that he was just above his head!

He heard Julian scrabble about in the path, and then drop the big stone back into its place. He watched the light of Julian's torch bobbing back up the path to the kitchen door. Then the door shut with a bang.

And now Dick could hardly breathe! Who would come for the parcel? He listened, stiff with excitement. The wind blew and a leaf rustled against the back of his neck making him jump. It felt as if a finger had touched him.

Five minutes went by and nobody came. Then he heard the slightest sound. Was that somebody crawling through the hedge? Dick strained his eyes but could only make out a deeper shadow that seemed to be moving. Then he could most distinctly hear somebody breathing hard as they tugged at the heavy stone! The parcel was being collected as arranged!

The stone plopped back. A shadow crept over to the hedge again. Whoever had the parcel was now going off with it.

Dick dropped quietly down. He had rubber shoes on and made no noise. He slipped through a big gap in the hedge nearby and stood straining his eyes to find the man he wanted to follow. Ah – there was a shadow moving steadily down the field-path to the stile. Dick followed, keeping close to the hedge.

He kept well behind the moving shadow till it reached the stile, got over it and went into the lane beyond. When it got there it stopped, and a perfect fusillade of loud owl-hoots came to Dick's startled ears.

Of course! That was the signal that the parcel had been collected. Dick admired the excellent imitation of a little owl's loud, excited hooting.

The shadow stopped hooting and went on again. It obviously did not suspect that it might be followed and, although it moved quietly, it did not attempt to keep under cover. Down the lane it went and into a field.

Dick was about to follow when he heard the sound of voices. They were very low, and he couldn't hear a word. He crouched in the shadow of the gate, which was swung right back, leaving an entry into the field.

A loud noise made him jump. Then a brilliant light dazzled him and he felt glad he could duck down behind the gate. There was a car in the field. A car that had just started up its engine and switched on its lights. It was going, moving slowly down to the gate!

Dick tried his hardest to see who was in the car. He could make out only one man, and he was driving. It didn't seem as if anyone else was in the car at all. Where was the other fellow, then – the one who must have collected the parcel and given it to the man in the car? Had he been left behind? If so, Dick had better be careful!

The car was soon out in the lane. It gained speed and then Dick heard it roaring off in the distance. He couldn't stalk a car, that was certain! He held his breath, listening for some movement of the other man who, he felt certain, was still there.

He heard a sniff and crouched lower still. Then a shadow passed quickly through the gate, turned back in the direction of Kirrin Cottage and was lost in the darkness of the lane.

In a trice Dick was after it again. At least he could track down *this* fellow! He must be going somewhere!

Down the lane to the stile. Over the stile and into the field. Across the field and back at the hedge that grew at the bottom of Kirrin Cottage.

Why was this fellow going back there? Dick was puzzled. He heard the shadow creeping through the hedge and he followed. He watched it go silently up the path and peer in at a darkened window.

'Going to get into the house again and ransack it, I suppose!' thought Dick, in a rage. He considered the shadowy figure by the window. It didn't look big. It must be a small man – one that Dick could tackle and bring to

the ground. He could yell loudly for Julian, and maybe he could hold the fellow down till Julian came.

'And then perhaps *we* could do a little kidnapping, and a little bargaining, too,' thought Dick grimly. 'If *they* hold George as a hostage, we'll hold one of them, too! Tit for tat!'

He waited till the shadow left the window, and then he pounced. His victim went down at once with a yell.

Dick was surprised how small he was – but how he fought! He bit and scratched and heaved and kicked, and the two of them rolled over and over and over, breaking down Michaelmas daisies in the beds, and scratching legs and arms and faces on rose bushes. Dick yelled for Julian all the time.

'Julian! JULIAN! Help! JULIAN!'

Julian heard. He tore out at once. 'Dick, Dick, where are you? What is it?'

He flashed his torch towards the shouting and saw

Dick rolling on top of somebody. He ran to help at once, throwing his torch on the grass so that both hands were free.

It wasn't long before they had the struggling figure firmly in their grasp and dragged it, wailing, to the back door. Dick recognized that wailing voice! Good gracious – no, it couldn't be – it couldn't be Jo!

But it was! When they dragged her inside she collapsed completely, sobbing and wailing, rubbing her scratched and bruised legs, calling both boys all the names she could think of. Anne and Joan looked on in complete amazement. *Now* what had happened?

'Put her upstairs,' said Julian. 'Get her to bed. She's in a awful state now. So am I! I wouldn't have lammed her like that if I'd known it was only Jo.'

'I never guessed,' said Dick, wiping his filthy face with his handkerchief. 'My word, what a wild-cat! See how she's bitten me!'

'I didn't know it was you, Dick; I didn't know,' wailed Jo. 'You pounced on me, and I fought back. I wouldn't have bitten you like that.'

'You're a savage, deceitful, double-dealing little wild-cat,' said Dick, looking at his bites and scratches. 'Pretending you know nothing about the man who gave you that note – and all the time you're in with that crooked lot of thieves and kidnappers, whoever they are.'

'I'm not in with them,' wept Jo.

'Don't tell lies,' shouted Dick, in a fury. 'I was up in a tree when you came and took that parcel from under the stone – yes, and I followed you right to that car – and followed you back again! You came back here to steal again, I suppose?'

Jo gulped. 'No, I didn't.'

'You did! You'll be handed over to the police to-morrow,' said Dick, still furious.

'I *didn't* come back to steal. I came back for something else,' insisted Jo, her eyes peering through her tangled hair like a frightened animal's.

'Ho! So you say! And what did you come back for? To find another dog to dope?' jeered Dick.

'No,' said Jo, miserably. 'I came back to tell you I'd take you to where George was, if you wouldn't tell on me. My Dad would half kill me if he thought I'd split on him. I know I took the parcel – I had to. I didn't know what it was or anything. I took it to the place I was told to. Jake told me. And then I came back to tell you all I could. And you set on me like that.'

Four pairs of eyes bored into Jo, and she covered her face. Dick took her hands away and made her look at him.

'Look here,' he said, 'this matters a lot to us, whether you are speaking the truth or not. Do you know where George is?'

Jo nodded.

'And will you take us there?' said Julian, his voice stern and cold.

Jo nodded again. 'Yes I will. You've been mean to me, but I'll show you I'm not as bad as you make out. I'll take you to George.'

Chapter Twelve

JO BEGINS TO TALK

THE hall clock suddenly struck loudly. DONG!'

'One o'clock,' said Joan. 'One o'clock in the morning! Master Julian, we can't do any more tonight. This gipsy child here, she's not fit to take you trapesing out anywhere else. She's done for – she can hardly stand.'

'Yes, you're right Joan,' said Julian, at once giving up the idea of going out to find George that night. 'We'll have to wait till tomorrow. It's a pity the telphone wires are cut. I do really think we ought to let the police know something about all this.'

Jo looked up at once. 'Then I won't tell you where George is,' she said. 'Do you know what the police will do to me if they get hold of me? They'll put me into a Home for Bad Girls, and I'll never get out again – because I *am* a bad girl and I do bad things. I've never had a chance.'

'Every one gets a chance sooner or later,' said Julian gently. 'You'll get yours, Jo – but see you take it when it comes. All right – we'll leave the police out of it if you promise you'll take us to where George is. That's a bargain.'

Jo understood bargains. She nodded. Joan pulled her to her feet and half led, half carried her upstairs.

'There's a couch in my room,' she told Julian. 'She can bed down there for the night – but late or not she's going to have a bath first. She smells like something the dog brought in!'

In half an hour's time Jo was tucked up on the couch in Joan's room, perfectly clean, though marked with scratches and bruises from top to toe, hair washed, dried, and brushed so that it stood up in wiry curls like George's. A basin of steaming bread and milk was on a tray in front of her.

Joan went to the landing and called across to Julian's room. 'Master Julian! Jo's in bed. She wants to say something to you and Master Dick.'

Dick and Julian put on dressing-gowns and went into Joan's neat room. They hardly recognized Jo. She was wearing one of Anne's old nightgowns and looked very clean and childish and somehow pathetic.

Jo looked at them and gave them a very small smile. 'What do you want to say to us?' asked Julian.

'I've got some things to tell you,' said Jo, stirring the bread round and round in the basin. 'I feel good now – good and clean and – and all that. But maybe tomorrow I'll feel like I always do – and then I wouldn't tell you everything. So I'd better tell you now.'

'Go ahead,' said Julian.

'Well, I let the men into your house here, the night they came,' said Jo. Julian and Dick stared in astonishment. Jo went on stirring her bread round and round.

'It's true,' she said. 'I got in at that tiny window that was left unfastened, and then I went to the back door and opened it and let the men in. They did make a mess of that room, didn't they? I watched them. They took a lot of papers.'

'You couldn't possibly squeeze through that window,' said Dick at once.

'Well, I did,' said Jo. 'I've – I've squeezed through quite a lot of little windows. I know how to wriggle, you see. I can't get through such tiny ones as I used to, because I keep on growing. But yours was easy.'

'Phew!' said Julian, and let out a long breath. He hardly knew what to say. 'Well, go on. I suppose when the men had finished you locked and bolted the kitchen door after them and then squeezed out of the pantry window again?'

'Yes,' said Jo, and put a piece of milky bread into her mouth.

'What about Timmy? Who doped him so that he slept all that night?' demanded Dick.

'I did,' said Jo. 'That was easy, too.'

Both boys were speechless. To think that Jo did that, too! The wicked little misery!

'I made friends with Timmy on the beach, don't you remember?' said Jo. 'George was cross about it. I like dogs. We always had dozens till Mum died, and they'd do anything I told them. Dad told me what I was to do – make friends with Timmy so that I could meet him that night and give him meat with something in it.'

'I see. And it was very, very easy, because we sent Timmy out alone – straight into your hands,' said Dick bitterly.

'Yes. He came to me at once, he was glad to see me. I took him quite a long walk, letting him sniff the meat I'd got. When I gave it to him, he swallowed it all at once with hardly a chew!'

'And slept all night long so that your precious friends could break into the house,' said Julian. 'All I can say is that you are a hardened little rogue. Aren't you ashamed of anything?'

'I don't know,' said Jo, who wasn't really quite certain what feeling ashamed meant. 'Shall I stop telling you things?'

'No. For goodness' sake go on,' said Dick, hastily. 'Had you anything to do with George's kidnapping?'

'I just had to hoot like an owl when she and Timmy were coming,' said Jo. 'They were ready for her with a sack to put over her head – and they were going to bang Timmy on the head with a stick to knock him out – then put him into a sack too. That's what I heard them say. But I didn't see them. I had to creep back here and shut the front door, so that if nobody missed George till morning they'd just think she'd gone out early somewhere.'

'Which is what we did think,' groaned Dick. 'What mutts we are! The only clever thing we thought of was to stalk the person who collected the parcel.'

'It was only me, though,' said Jo. 'And anyway, I was coming back to tell you I would take you to George. Not because I like her – I don't. I think she's rude and horrible. I'd like her to stay kidnapped for years!'

'What a nice, kind nature!' said Julian to Dick, helplessly. 'What can you do with a kid like this?' He turned to Jo again. 'Seeing that you wish George would stay kidnapped for years, what made you decide to come and tell us where to find her?' he asked, puzzled.

'Well, I don't like George – but I do like *him*!' said Jo, pointing with her spoon at Dick. 'He was nice to me, so I wanted to be nice back. I don't often feel like that,' she added hurriedly, as if being kind was some sort of weakness not really to be admired. 'I wanted him to go on liking me,' she said.

Dick looked at her. 'I shall like you if you take us to George,' he said. 'Not unless. If you deceive us, I shall think you're like one of those sour damson stones – only fit to be spat out as far away as possible.'

'I'll take you tomorrow,' said Jo.

'Where *is* George?' asked Julian, bluntly, thinking it would be as well to know now, in case Jo changed her mind by the morning, and became her wicked little self again.

Jo hesitated. She looked at Dick. 'It would be very nice of you to tell us,' said Dick, in a kind voice. Jo loved a bit of kindness and couldn't resist this.

'Well,' she whispered, 'you know I told you my Dad had gone off and left me to Jake. Dad didn't tell me why – but Jake did. He shut George and Timmy into our caravan, harnessed Blackie the horse, and drove away in the night with them both. And I guess I know where he's gone – where he always goes when he wants to hide.'

'Where?' asked Julian, feeling so astounded at these extraordinary revelations that he really began to wonder if he was dreaming.

'In the middle of Ravens Wood,' said Jo. 'You don't know where that is, but I do. I'll take you tomorrow. I can't tell you any more now.' She began to spoon up her bread and milk very fast indeed, watching the boys through her long eyelashes.

Dick considered her. He felt pretty sure she had told them the truth, though he was equally certain she would have told lies if she could have got more by doing so.

He thought her a bad, cold-blooded, savage little monkey, but he pitied her, and admired her unwillingly for her courage.

He caught sight of her bruises and grazes, and bit his lip as he remembered how he had pounced on her and pummelled her, giving her back kick for kick and blow for blow – he hadn't guessed for one moment it was Jo.

'I'm sorry I hurt you so,' he said. 'You know I didn't mean to. It was a mistake.'

Jo looked at him as a slave might look at a king. 'I don't mind,' she said. 'I'd do anything for you, straight I would. You're kind.'

Joan knocked impatiently at the door. 'Aren't you ready yet, you boys?' she said. 'I want to come to bed. Tell Jo to stop talking, and you come on out too, and go to bed.'

The boys opened the door. Joan took one look at their solemn faces and guessed that what Jo had told them was important. She took the empty basin from the girl's hands and pushed her down on the couch.

'Now you go straight off to sleep – and mind, if I hear any hanky-panky from you in the night I'll get up and give you such a spanking you won't be able to sit down for a month of Sundays,' she said roughly, but not unkindly.

Jo grinned. She understood that kind of talk. She snuggled down into the rugs, marvelling at the warmth and softness. She was already half-asleep. Joan got into bed and switched off her light.

'Two o'clock in the morning!' she muttered as she heard the hall clock strike. 'Such goings-on! I'll never wake up in time to tell the milkman I want more milk.'

Soon only Julian was awake. He worried about whether he was doing right or not. Poor George – was she safe? Would that scamp of a Jo really lead them to the caravan next day – or might she lead them right into the lion's mouth, and get them all captured? Julian simply didn't know.

Chapter Thirteen

OFF TO FIND GEORGE

JOAN was the only one in the household who woke up reasonably early the next morning – but even she was too late to catch the milkman. She scurried downstairs at half-past seven, an hour later than usual, tying up her apron as she went.

'Half-past seven – what a time to wake up!' she muttered, as she began to do the kitchen fire. She thought of all the happenings of the night before – the queer evening with young Sid, Dick's capture of Jo – and Jo's extraordinary tale. She had had a look at Jo before she went down, half expecting that lively young rogue to have disappeared in the night.

But Jo was curled up like a kitten, her brown cheek on her brown paw, her hair, unusually bright and tidy, falling over her tightly-shut eyes. She didn't even stir when Joan scurried about the bedroom, washing and dressing.

The others were fast asleep, too. Julian woke first, but not till eight o'clock. He remembered immediately all that had happened, and jumped out of bed at once.

He went to Joan's room. He could hear Joan downstairs talking to herself as usual. He peeped round the open door of her bedroom. Thank goodness – Jo was still there.

He went and shook her gently. She wriggled away, turned over and buried her face in the pillow. Julian shook her more vigorously. He meant to get her up and make her take them to where George was as soon as possible!

Most miraculously everyone was down at half-past eight, eating porridge and looking rather subdued. Jo had hers in the kitchen, and the others could hear Joan scolding her for her manners.

'Have you got to stuff yourself like that, as if the dog's going to come and lick your plate before you've finished? And who told you to stick your fingers into the syrup and lick them? I've eyes in the back of my head, so just you be careful what you're doing!'

Jo liked Joan. She knew where she was with her. If she kept on Joan's right side and did what she was told, Joan would feed her well and not interfere too much – but if she didn't, then she could expect something else she understood very well indeed – scoldings and a sharp slap. Joan was good-hearted but impatient, and no child was ever afraid of her. Jo followed her about like a little dog when she had finished her breakfast.

Julian came out into the kitchen at nine o'clock. 'Where's Jo?' he said. 'Oh, there you are. Now, what about taking us to where you father's caravan is? You're sure you know the way?'

Jo laughed scornfully. 'Course I do! I know everywhere round here for miles.'

'Right,' said Julian, and he produced a map, which he spread out on the kitchen table. He put a finger on one spot. 'That's Kirrin,' he said. 'And here's a place called

Ravens Wood. Is that the place you mean? How do you
propose to get there – by this road, or that one?'

Jo looked at the map. It meant nothing to her at all.
She gazed vaguely at the spot that Julian had pointed to.

'Well?' said Julian, impatiently. 'Is that the Ravens
Wood you mean?'

'I don't know,' said Jo, helplessly. 'The one I mean is a real wood – I don't know anything about yours on this map.'

Joan gave a little snort. 'Master Julian, maps are wasted on her. I don't expect she's ever seen one in her life! She can't even read!'

'*Can't* she?' said Julian, amazed. 'Then she can't write either.' He looked questioningly at Jo.

She shook her head. 'Mum tried to learn me to read,' she said, 'but Mum wasn't very good herself. What's the good of reading, anyway? Won't help you to trap rabbits or catch fish for your dinner, will it?'

'No. It's used for other things,' said Julian, amused. 'Well – maps are no good to *you*, I can see.' He rolled his map up, looking thoughtful. It was very difficult to know exactly how to deal with a person like Jo, who knew so little of some things and so much of others.

'She'll know the way all right,' said Joan, scraping out a saucepan. 'They're like dogs, these folk – they can smell out any road they want.'

'*Do* you smell out your way like a dog?' asked Anne, curiously. She had come in to see what was going on, and was quite willing to believe that Jo really could smell her way here and there, as Timmy did.

'No, I don't,' said Jo. 'I just know the way I have to go. And I don't go by the roads, either! They take too long to get to a place. I take the shortest way, see?'

'How do you know it's the shortest way?' asked Anne.

Jo shrugged her thin shoulders. All this was very boring to her.

'Where's that other boy?' she said. 'Isn't he coming? I want to see him.'

'She's just crazy on Dick,' said Joan, taking up another saucepan. 'Here he is – now you can go and lick his boots if you want to, young Jo!'

'Hallo, Jo!' said Dick, with one of his amiable grins. 'Ready to take us travelling?'

'Better go at night,' said Jo, staring at Dick.

'Oh, no!' said Dick. 'We're going *now*. We're not going to be put off like that. *Now*, Jo, now!'

'If my Dad sees us coming he'll be mad,' said Jo obstinately.

'Very well,' said Dick, looking at Julian. 'We'll go by ourselves. We've found Ravens Wood on the map. We can easily get there.'

'Pooh,' said Jo, rudely. 'You can get there all right – but it's a big place, Ravens Wood is – and nobody but me and Dad knows where we hide the caravan there. And if Dad wants to keep George quite safe, he'll take her to our hidey-hole in the middle of the wood, see? You can't go without me.'

'Right. Then we'll get the police to take us,' said Julian, quite cheerfully. 'They will help us to comb the wood from end to end. We'll soon find George.'

'No!' cried Jo, in alarm. 'You said you wouldn't! You promised!'

'*You* made a promise too,' said Julian. 'It was a bargain. But I see you're not really to be trusted. I'll just get on my bike and ride down to the police-station.'

But before he could go out of the room Jo flung herself

on him and clung to his arm like a cat. 'No, no! I'll take you. I'll keep my promise! But it *would* be best to go at night!'

'I'm not putting things off any more,' said Julian, shaking Jo off his arm. 'If you mean what you say, you'll come with us now. Make up your mind.'

'I'll come,' said Jo.

'Hadn't we better give her another pair of shorts or something?' said Anne, suddenly seeing a tremendous hole in Jo's grubby shorts. 'She can't go out like that. And look at her awful jersey. It's full of holes.'

The boys looked at it. 'She'd smell a bit better if she had clean clothes,' said Joan. 'There's that old pair of shorts I washed for George last week, and mended up. Jo could have those. And there's an old shirt of hers she could have, too.'

In five minutes' time Jo was proudly wearing a pair of perfectly clean, much-mended shorts of George's, and a shirt like the one Anne had on. Anne looked at her and laughed.

'Now she's more like George than ever! They might be sisters.'

'Brothers, you mean,' said Dick. 'George and Jo – what a pair!'

Jo scowled. She didn't like George, and she didn't want to look like her.

'She's even got George's scowl!' said Anne. Jo turned her back at once, and Joan then got the benefit of the scowl.

'My word, what an ugly creature you are!' said Joan.

'You be careful the wind doesn't change – you might get your face stuck like that!'

'Oh, come on,' said Julian, impatiently. 'Jo! Do you hear me? Come along now and take us to Ravens Wood.'

'Jake might see us,' said Jo, sulkily. She was determined to put off going as long as she could.

'Yes, he might,' said Julian, who hadn't thought of that. 'Well – you go on a long way ahead, and we'll follow. We won't let Jake know you're leading us anywhere.'

At last they set off. Joan had packed them up a meal in case they wanted one. Julian slipped the package into a bag and slid it over his shoulder.

Jo slipped out the back way, went down to the bottom of the garden and made her way out to the lane through a little thicket. The others went out of the front gate and walked up the lane slowly, watching for Jo to appear.

'There she is,' said Julian. 'Come on. We must keep the little wretch in sight. I wouldn't be surprised if she gave us the slip even now!'

Jo danced on in front, a good way ahead. She took no notice of the others behind, and they followed steadily.

Then suddenly something happened. A dark figure strode out from the hedge, stood in front of Jo, and said something to her. She screamed and tried to dodge away. But the man caught hold of her and firmly pulled her into the hedge.

'It was Jake!' said Dick. 'I'm sure it was Jake. He was watching out for her. *Now* what do we do?'

Chapter Fourteen

SIMMY'S CARAVAN

THEY all hurried up to the place where Jake had caught hold of Jo. There was absolutely nothing to be seen except a few broken twigs in the hedge there. No Jake, no Jo. There was not a sound to be heard, either. Not a scream from Jo, not a shout from Jake. It was as if both had faded into the hedge and disappeared.

Dick squeezed through the hedge and into the field beyond. Nobody was there either, except a few cows who looked at him in surprise, their tails whisking.

'There's a little copse at the end of the field,' called back Dick. 'I bet they're there. I'll go and see.'

He ran across the field to the copse. But there was nobody there either. Beyond the copse was a row of huddled-up cottages. Dick looked along the untidy row, exasperated.

'I suppose Jake's taken her to one of those,' he thought, angrily. 'Probably lives there! Well, he won't let her go, that's certain. He most likely guesses that she's in with us now. Poor Jo!'

He went back to the others and they had a low-voiced conference in the lane. 'Let's tell the police now,' begged Anne.

'No. Let's go to Ravens Wood ourselves,' said Dick. 'We know where it is. We wouldn't be able to go the way Jo would have taken us – but at least we can go by the map.'

'Yes. I think we will,' said Julian. 'Come on, then. Quick march!'

They went on up the lane, took a field path and came out eventually on to a road. A bus passed them in the opposite direction to which they were going.

'When we come to a bus stop we'll find out if one goes anywhere near Raven's Wood,' said Julian. 'It would save a lot of time if we caught a bus. We'd be there long before Jake, if he thinks of going to warn Jo's father we're on the way! I bet Jo will tell him. You might as well trust a snake as that slippery little thing.'

'I hate Jo!' said Anne, almost in tears. 'I don't trust her a bit. Do you, Dick?'

'I don't know,' said Dick. 'I can't make up my mind. She hasn't really proved whether she's trustable or not yet. Anyway, she came back to tell us all she knew last night, didn't she?'

'I don't believe she *did* come back for that,' said Anne obstinately. 'I believe she was coming back to pry and snoop.'

'You may be right,' said Dick. 'Look, here's a bus-stop – and a time-table!'

A bus did apparently go quite near Ravens Wood, and was due in five minutes' time. They sat down on the bus-stop seat and waited. The bus was punctual and came rumbling down the road, full of women going to Ravens

Market. They all seemed very plump women and had enormous baskets, so it was difficult to squeeze inside.

Everyone got out at Ravens Market. Julian asked his way to Ravens Wood. 'There it is,' said the conductor, pointing down the hill to where trees grew thickly in the valley. 'It's a big place. Don't get lost! And look out for the gipsies. There's usually hordes of them there!'

'Thanks,' said Julian, and the three of them set off down the hill into the valley. They came to the wood.

'It's a proper wood,' said Anne. 'Nothing but trees and trees. I should think it gets very thick in the middle – like a forest.'

They came to a clearing where there was a little gipsy camp. Three rather dirty-looking caravans stood together, and a crowd of brown gipsy children were playing some sort of a game with a rope. Julian took a quick look at the caravans. All had their doors open.

'No George here,' he said in a low voice to the others. 'I wish I knew exactly where to go! I suppose if we follow this broad pathway it would be best. After all, Jo's caravan must have a fairly broad way to go on.'

'Can't we ask if anyone knows if Jo's caravan is anywhere about?' said Anne.

'We don't know her father's name,' said Julian.

'But we could say it's a caravan drawn by a horse called Blackie, and that a girl called Jo lives in it with her father,' said Anne.

'Yes. I'd forgotten the horse,' said Julian. He went up to an old woman who was stirring something in a black pot over a fire of sticks. Julian thought she looked very like a witch. She peered up at him through tangled grey hair.

'Can you tell me if there's a caravan in the wood drawn by a horse called Blackie?' he asked politely. 'A girl called Jo lives in it with her father. We want to see her.'

The old woman blinked. She took an iron spoon out of the pot and waved it to the right.

'Simmy's gone down-away there,' she said. 'I never saw Jo this time – but the caravan door was shut so maybe she was inside. What you want with Jo?'

'Oh – only just to see her,' said Julian, quite unable to think up a good reason for going to visit a gipsy-child on the spur of the moment. 'Is Simmy her father?'

The old woman nodded and began to stir her pot again. Julian went back to the others.

'This way,' he said, and they went down the rutted path. It was just wide enough for a caravan to go down. Anne looked up. Tree branches waved overhead.

'I should think they brush against the roof of a caravan all the time,' she said. 'What a queer life to live – in a little caravan day in and day out, hiding yourself away in woods and fields!'

They walked on down the path, which wound about through the trees, following the clear spaces. Sometimes the trees were so close together that it seemed impossible for a caravan to go between. But the wheel-ruts showed that caravans did go down the path.

After a time the wood became thicker, and the sunlight could hardly pierce through the branches. Still the path went on, but now it seemed as if only one set of wheel-ruts was marked on it. They were probably the wheels of Simmy's caravan.

Here and there a tree was shorn of one of its branches, and a bush uprooted and thrown to one side.

'Simmy meant to go deep into the wood last time he came,' said Julian, pointing to where a bush lay dying by the side of the path. 'He's cleared the way here and there. Actually we aren't on a proper path any longer – we're only following wheel-ruts.'

It was true. The path had faded out. They were now

in a thick part of the wood, with only the ruts of the caravan wheels to guide them.

They fell silent. The wood was very quiet. There were no birds singing, and the branches of the trees were so thick that there was a kind of green twilight round them.

'I wish we had Timmy with us,' half-whispered Anne at last.

Julian nodded. He had been wishing that a long time. He was also wishing he hadn't brought Anne – but when they had started out, they had Jo with them to guide them, and warn them of any danger. Now they hadn't.

'I think we'd better go very cautiously,' he said, in a low voice. 'We may come on the caravan unexpectedly. We don't want Simmy to hear us and lie in wait.'

'I'll go a little way in front and warn you if I hear or see anything,' said Dick. Julian nodded to him and he went on ahead, peering round the trees when he came to any curve in the wheel-rut path. Julian began to think of what they would do when they reached the caravan. He was pretty certain that both George and Timmy would be found locked up securely inside.

'If we can undo the door and let them out, Timmy will do the rest,' he thought. 'He's as good as three policemen! Yes – that's the best plan.'

Dick suddenly stopped and lifted up his hand in warning. He peered round the bole of a big tree, and then turned and nodded excitedly.

'He's found the caravan!' said Anne, and her heart began its usual thump-thump-thump of excitement.

'Stay here,' said Julian to Anne, and went on quietly

to join Dick. Anne crept under a bush. She didn't like this dark, silent wood, with the green light all round. She peered out, watching the boys.

Dick had suddenly seen the caravan. It was small, badly needed painting, and appeared quite deserted. No fire burned outside. No Simmy was sitting anywhere about. Not even Blackie the horse was to be seen.

The boys watched intently for a few minutes, not daring to move or speak. There was absolutely no sound or movement from the tiny clearing in which the caravan stood.

Windows and doors were shut. The shafts rested crookedly on the ground. The whole place seemed deserted.

'Dick,' whispered Julian at last, 'Simmy doesn't seem to be about. This is our chance! We'll creep over to the caravan and look into the window. We'll attract George's attention, and get her out as soon as we can. Timmy, too.'

'Funny he doesn't bark,' said Dick, also in a whisper. 'I suppose he can't have heard us. Well – shall we get over to the caravan now?'

They ran quietly to the little caravan, and Julian peered through the dirty window. It was too dark inside to see anything at all.

'George!' he whispered. 'George! Are you there?'

Chapter Fifteen

ANNE DOESN'T LIKE ADVENTURES

THERE was no answer from inside the caravan. Perhaps
George was asleep – or drugged! And Timmy, too.
Julian's heart sank. It would be dreadful if George had
been ill-treated. He tried to peer inside the window again,
but what with the darkness of the wood and the dirt on
the pane, it really was impossible to see inside.

'Shall we bang on the door?' asked Dick.

'No. That would only bring Simmy if he's anywhere
about – and if George is inside and awake, our voices
would have attracted her attention,' said Julian.

They went quietly round the carvan to the door at
the back. It had no key in the lock. Julian frowned.

Simmy must have got the key with him. That would
mean breaking down the door and making a noise. He
went up the few steps and pushed at the door. It seemed
very solid indeed. How could he break it down, anyway?
He had no tools, and it didn't look as if kicking and
shoving would burst it in.

He knocked gently on the door – rap-rap-rap. Not a
movement from inside. It seemed very strange. He tried
the round handle, and it turned easily.

It not only turned easily – but the door opened! 'Dick! It's not locked!' said Julian, forgetting to whisper in his surprise. He went inside the dark caravan, hardly hoping now to see George or Timmy.

Dick pushed in after him. There was a nasty sour smell and it was very untidy. Nobody was there. It was quite empty, as Julian had feared.

He groaned. 'All this way for nothing. They've taken George somewhere else. We're done, now, Dick – we haven't a clue where to go next.'

Dick fished his torch out of his pocket. He flashed it over the untidy jumble of things in the caravan, looking for some sign that George had been there. But there was nothing at all that he could see to show him that either Timmy or George had been there.

'It's quite likely that Jo made the whole story up about her father taking George away,' he groaned. 'It doesn't look as if they've been here at all.'

His torch flashed on to the wooden wall of the caravan, and Dick saw something that arrested his attention. Somebody had written something on the wall!

He looked more closely. 'Julian! Isn't that George's writing? Look! What's written there?'

Both boys bent towards the dirty wall. 'Red Tower, Red Tower, Red Tower,' was written again and again, in very small writing.

'Red Tower!' said Dick. 'What does that mean? *Is* it George's writing?'

'Yes, I think so,' said Julian. 'But why should she keep writing that? Do you suppose that's where they have taken her to? She might have heard them saying something and scribbled it down quickly – just in *case* we found the caravan and examined it. Red Tower! It sounds queer.'

'It must be a house with a red tower, I should think,' said Dick. 'Well – we'd better get back and tell the police now – and they'll have to hunt for a red tower somewhere.'

Bitterly disappointed the boys went back to Anne. She scrambled out from under her bush as they came.

'George is not there,' said Dick. 'She's gone. But she *has* been there – we saw some scribbled writing on the wall of the caravan inside.'

'How do you know it's hers?' said Anne.

'Well, she's written "Red Tower" ever so many times, and the R's and the T's are just like hers,' said Dick. 'We think she must have heard someone talking and say they were taking her to Red Tower, wherever it is. We're going straight back to the police now. I wish we hadn't trusted Jo. We've wasted such a lot of time.'

'Let's have something to eat,' said Julian. 'We won't sit down. We'll eat as we go. Come on.'

But somehow nobody wanted anything to eat. Anne said she felt sick. Julian was too worried to eat, and Dick was so anxious to go that he felt he couldn't even wait to unpack sandwiches! So they started back down the path, following the wheel-ruts as before.

It suddenly grew very dark indeed, and on the leaves of the trees heavy rain fell with a loud, pattering sound. Thunder suddenly rolled.

Anne caught hold of Julian's arm, startled. 'Julian! It's dangerous to be in a wood, isn't it, in a storm? Oh, Julian, we'll be struck by lightning.'

'No, we shan't,' said Julian. 'A wood's no more dangerous than anywhere else. It's sheltering under a lone tree somewhere that's dangerous. Look – there's a little clearing over there; we'll go to that, if you like.'

But when they got to the little clearing the rain was falling down in such heavy torrents that Julian could see that they would immediately be soaked through. He hurried Anne to a clump of bushes, and they crouched underneath, waiting for the storm to pass.

Soon the rain stopped, and the thunder rolled away to the east. There had been no lightning that they could see. The wood grew just a little lighter, as if somewhere above the thick green branches the sun might be shining!

'I hate this wood,' said Dick, crawling out from the bushes. 'Come on, for goodness' sake. Let's get back to the wheel-rut path.'

He led the way through the trees. Julian called to him. 'Wait, Dick. Are you sure this is right?'

Dick stopped, anxious at once. 'Well,' he said uncertainly. 'I thought it was. But I don't know. Do you?'

'*I* thought it was through those trees there,' said Julian. 'Where that little clearing is.'

They went to it. 'It's not the same clearing, though,' said Anne at once. 'The other clearing had a dead tree at one side. There's no dead tree here.'

'Blow!' said Julian. 'Well – try *this* way, then.'

They went to the left, and soon found themselves in a

thicker part of the wood than ever. Julian's heart went cold. What an absolute idiot he was! He might have known that it was madness to leave the only path they knew without marking it in some way.

Now he hadn't the very faintest idea where the wheel-rut way was. It might be in any direction! He hadn't even the sun to guide him.

He looked gloomily at Dick. 'Bad show!' said Dick. 'Well – we'll have to make up our minds which way to go! We can't just stay here.'

'We might go deeper and deeper and deeper,' said Anne, with a sudden little gulp of fear. Julian put his arm round her shoulder.

'Well, if we go deeper and deeper, we shall come out on the other side!' he said. 'It's not an endless wood, you know.'

'Well, let's go straight on through the wood, then,' said Anne. 'We'll *have* to come out the other side some time.'

The boys didn't tell her that it was impossible to go straight through a wood. It was necessary to go round clumps of bushes, to double back sometimes when they came to an impenetrable part, and to go either to the left or right when clumps of trees barred their way. It was quite impossible to go *straight* through.

'For all I know we're probably going round and round in circles, like people do when they're lost in the desert,' he thought. He blamed himself bitterly for having left the wheel-ruts.

They made their way on and on for about two or three

hours, and then Anne stumbled and fell. 'I can't go on any further,' she wept. 'I must have a rest.'

Dick glanced at his watch and whistled. Where ever had the time gone? It was almost three o'clock. He sat down by Anne and pulled her close to him. 'What we want is a jolly good meal,' he said. 'We've had nothing since breakfast.'

Anne said she still wasn't hungry, but when she smelt the meat sandwiches that Joan had made she changed her mind. She was soon eating with the others, and feeling much better.

'There's nothing to drink, unfortunately,' said Dick. 'But Joan's packed tomatoes and plums, too – so we'll have those instead of a drink. They're nice and juicy.'

They ate everything, though secretly Julian wondered if it was a good thing to wolf all their food at once. There was no telling how long they might be lost in Ravens Wood! Joan might get worried sooner or later and tell the police they had gone there, and a search would be made. But it might be ages before they were found.

Anne fell asleep after her meal. The boys talked softly over her head. 'I don't much like this,' said Dick. 'We set out to find George – and all we've done is to lose ourselves. We don't seem to be managing this adventure as well as we usually do.'

'If we don't get out before dark we'll have to make up some kind of bed under a bush,' said Julian. 'We'll have another go when Anne wakes – and we'll do a bit of yelling, too. Then if we're still lost, we'll bed down for the night.'

But when darkness came – and it came very early in that thick wood, they were still as much lost as ever. They were all hoarse with shouting, too.

In silence they pulled bracken from an open space and piled it under a sheltering bush. 'Thank goodness it's warm tonight,' said Dick, trying to sound cheerful. 'Well – we'll all feel much more lively in the morning. Cuddle up to me, Anne, and keep warm. That's right. Julian's on the other side of you! This is quite an adventure.'

'I don't like adventures,' said Anne, in a small voice, and immediately fell asleep.

Chapter Sixteen

VISITOR IN THE NIGHT

IT took a long time for Julian and Dick to fall asleep. They were both worried – worried about George and worried about themselves, too. They were also very hungry, and their hunger kept them awake as much as their anxiety.

Dick fell asleep at last. Julian still lay awake, hoping that Anne was nice and warm between them. He didn't feel very warm himself.

He heard the whisper of the leaves in the trees, and then the scamper of tiny paws behind his head. He wondered what animal it was – a mouse?

Something ran lightly over his hair and he shivered. A spider, perhaps. Well he couldn't move, or he would disturb Anne. If it wanted to make a web over his hair it would have to. He shut his eyes and began to doze off. Soon he was dreaming.

He awoke very suddenly, with a jump. He heard the hoot of an owl. That must have been what wakened him. Now it would be ages before he slept again.

He shut his eyes. The owl hooted again and Julian frowned, hoping that Anne would not wake. She stirred and muttered in her sleep. Julian touched her lightly. She felt quite warm.

He settled down again and shut his eyes. Then he

opened them. He had heard something! Not an owl or the pattering of some little animal's feet – but another sound, a bigger one. He listened. There was a rustling going on somewhere. Some much bigger animal was about.

Julian was suddenly panic-stricken. Then he reasoned sternly with himself. There were no dangerous wild animals in this country, not even a wolf. It was probably a badger out on a nightly prowl. He listened for any snuffling sound, but he heard none, only the rustling as the animal moved about through the bushes.

It came nearer. It came right over to him! He felt warm breath on his ear and made a quick movement of revulsion. He sat up swiftly and put out his hand. It fell on something warm and hairy. He withdrew his hand at once, feeling for his torch in panic. To touch something warm and hairy in the pitch darkness was too much even for Julian!

Something caught hold of his arm, and he gave a yell and fought it off. Then he got the surprise of his life. The animal spoke.

'Julian!' said a voice. 'It's me!'

Julian, his hands trembling, flashed his torch round. The light fell on a dirty dark face, with tangled hair over its eyes.

'Jo!' said Julian. 'JO! What on earth are you doing here? You scared me stiff. I thought you were some horrible hairy animal. I must have touched your head.'

'You did,' said Jo, squeezing in under the bush. Anne and Dick, who had both wakened up at Julian's yell, gazed at her, speechless with surprise. Jo of all people, here in the middle of the wood. How had she got there?

'You're surprised to see me, aren't you?' said Jo. 'I got caught by Jake. But he didn't know you were following behind. He dragged me off to the cottage he lives in and locked me up. He knew I'd spent the night at Kirrin Cottage, and he said he was going to take me to my Dad, who would give me the worst hiding I'd ever had in my life. So he would, too.'

'So that's what happened to you!' said Dick.

'Then I broke the window and got out,' said Jo. 'That Jake! I'll never do a thing he tells me again – locking me up like that. I hate that worse than anything! Well, then I came to look for you.'

R—F

'How did you find us?' said Julian, in wonder.

'Well, first I went to the caravan,' said Jo. 'Old Ma Smith – the one who always sits stirring a pot – she told me you'd been asking for my Dad's caravan. I guessed you'd go off to find it. So along I went after you – but there was the caravan all by itself, and nobody there. Not even George.'

'Where *is* George, do you know?' asked Anne.

'No. I don't,' said Jo. 'Dad's taken her somewhere else. I expect he put her on Blackie, because Blackie's gone, too.'

'What about Timmy?' asked Dick.

Jo looked away. 'I reckon they've done Timmy in,' she said. Nobody said anything. The thought that Timmy might have come to harm was too dreadful to speak about.

'How did you find us here?' asked Julian at last.

'That was easy,' said Jo. 'I can follow anybody's trail. I'd have come quicker, but it got dark. My, you did wander round, didn't you?'

'Yes. We did,' said Dick. 'Do you mean to say you followed all our wanderings in and out and round about?'

'Oh, yes,' said Jo. 'Properly tired me out, you did, with all your messing round and round. Why did you leave the wheel-ruts?'

Julian told her. 'You're daft,' said Jo. 'If you're going somewhere off the path, just mark the trees with a nick as you go along – one here and one there – and then you can always find your way back.'

'We didn't even know we were lost till we were,' said Anne. She took Jo's hand and squeezed it. She was so very, very glad to see her. Now they would be able to get out of this horrible wood.

Jo was surprised and touched, but she withdrew her hand at once. She didn't like being fondled, though she would not have minded Dick taking her hand. Dick was her hero, someone above all others. He had been kind to her, and she was glad she had found him.

'We found something written on the caravan wall,' said Julian. 'We think we know where George has been taken. It's a place called Red Tower. Do you know it?'

'There's no place called Red Tower,' said Jo at once. 'It's . . .'

'Don't be silly, Jo. You can't possibly know if there's no place called Red Tower,' said Dick, impatiently. 'There may be hundreds of places with that name. That's the place we've got to find, anyway. The police will know it.'

Jo gave a frightened movement. 'You promised you wouldn't tell the police.'

'Yes – we promised that – but only if you took us to George,' said Dick. 'And you didn't. And anyway if you *had* taken us to the caravan George wouldn't have been there. So we'll jolly well have to call in the police now and find out where Red Tower is.'

'*Was* it Red Tower George had written down?' asked Jo. 'Well, then – I *can* take you to George!'

'How can you, when you say there's no place called Red Tower?' began Julian, exasperated. 'I don't believe a word you say, Jo. You're a fraud – and I half-believe you're still working for our enemies too!'

'I'm not,' said Jo. 'I'm NOT! You're mean. I tell you Red Tower isn't a place. Red Tower is a man.'

There was a most surprised silence after this astonishing remark. A man! Nobody had thought of that.

Jo spoke again, pleased at the surprise she had caused. 'His name's Tower, and he's got red hair, flaming red – so he's called Red Tower. See?'

'Are you making this up, by any chance?' asked Dick, after a pause. 'You have made up things before, you know.'

'All right. You can think I made it up, then,' said Jo, sulkily. 'I'll go. Get yourselves out of this the best you can. You're mean.'

She wriggled away, but Julian caught hold of her arm. 'Oh, no, you don't! You'll just stay with us now, if I have to tie you to me all night long! You see, we find it difficult to trust you, Jo – and that's your fault, not ours. But we'll trust you just this once. Tell us about Red Tower, and take us to where he lives. If you do that, we'll trust you for evermore.'

'Will Dick trust me, too?' said Jo, trying to get away from Julian's hand.

'Yes,' said Dick shortly. He felt as if he would dearly like to smack this unpredictable, annoying, extraordinary, yet somehow likeable ragamuffin girl. 'But I don't feel as if I *like* you very much at present. If you want us to like you as well as to trust you, you'll have to help us a lot more than you have done.'

'All right,' said Jo, and she wriggled down again. 'I'm

tired. I'll show you the way out in the morning, and then I'll take you to Red's. But you won't like Red. He's a beast.'

She would say nothing more, so once again they tried to sleep. They felt happier now that Jo was with them and would show them the right way out of the wood. Julian hardly thought she would leave them in the lurch now. He shut his eyes and was soon dreaming.

Jo woke first. She uncurled like an animal and stretched, forgetting where she was. She woke up the others, and they all sat up, feeling stiff, dirty and hungry.

'I'm thirsty as well as hungry,' complained Anne. 'Where can we get something to eat and drink?'

'Better get back home for a wash and a meal, and to let Joan know where we are,' said Julian. 'Come on, Jo – show us the way.'

Jo led the way immediately. The others wondered how in the world she knew it. They were even more astonished when they found themselves on the wheel-rut path in about two minutes.

'Gracious! We were as near to it as that!' said Dick. 'And yet we seemed to walk for miles through this horrible wood.'

'You did,' said Jo. 'You went round in an enormous circle, and you were almost back where you started. Come on – I'll take you *my* way back to your house now – it's much better than any bus!'

Chapter Seventeen

OFF IN GEORGE'S BOAT

JOAN was extremely thankful to see them. She had been so worried the night before that if the telephone wires in the house had been mended, she would most certainly have rung up the police. As it was, she couldn't telephone, and the night was so dark that she was really afraid of walking all the way down to the village.

'I haven't slept all night,' she declared. 'This mustn't happen again, Master Julian. It's worrying me to death. And now you haven't got George or Timmy. I tell you, if they don't turn up soon I'll take matters into my own hands. I haven't heard from your uncle and aunt either – let's hope they're not lost, too!'

She bustled about after this outburst, and was soon frying sausages and tomatoes for them. They couldn't wait till they were cooked, and helped themselves to great hunks of bread and butter.

'I can't even go and wash till I've had something,' said Anne. 'I'm glad you knew so many short cuts back here, Jo – the way didn't seem nearly so long as when we came by bus.'

It had really been amazing to see the deft, confident manner in which Jo had taken them home, through fields and little narrow paths, over stiles and across allotments. She was never once at a loss.

They had arrived not long after Joan had got up, and she had almost cried with surprise and relief when she had seen them walking up the front path.

'And a lot of dirty little tatterdemalions you looked,' she said, as she turned their breakfast out on to a big dish. 'And still do, for that matter. I'll get the kitchen fire going for a bath for you. You might all be sister and brothers to that ragamuffin Jo.'

Jo didn't mind remarks of this sort at all. She chewed her bread and grinned. She wolfed the breakfast with no manners at all – but the others were nearly as bad, they were so hungry!

'It's a spade and trowel you want for your food this morning, not a knife and fork,' said Joan, disapprovingly. 'You're just shovelling it in. No, I can't cook you any more, Master Julian. There's not a sausage left in the house nor a bit of bacon either. You fill up with toast and marmalade.'

The bath water ran vigorously after breakfast. All four had baths. Jo didn't want to, but Joan ran after her with a carpet beater, vowing and declaring she would beat the dust and dirt out of her if she didn't bath. So Jo bathed, and quite enjoyed it.

They had a conference after breakfast. 'About this fellow, Red Tower,' said Julian. 'Who is he, Jo? What do you know about him?'

'Not much,' said Jo. 'He's rich, and he talks queer, and I think he's mad. He gets fellows like Dad and Jake to do his dirty work for him.'

'What dirty work?' asked Dick.

'Oh – stealing and such,' said Jo, vaguely. 'I don't really know. Dad doesn't tell me much; I just do what I'm told, and don't ask questions. I don't want more slaps than I get!'

'Where does he live?' said Anne. 'Far away?'

'He's taken a house on the cliff,' said Jo. 'I don't know the way by land. Only by boat. It's a queer place – like a small castle almost, with very thick stone walls. Just the place for Red, my Dad says.'

'Have you been there?' asked Dick, eagerly.

Jo nodded. 'Oh, yes,' she said. 'Twice. My Dad took a big iron box there once, and another time he took something in a sack. I went with him.'

'Why?' asked Julian. 'I shouldn't have thought he'd wanted you messing round!'

'I rowed the boat,' said Jo. 'I told you, Red's place is up on the cliff. We got to it by boat; I don't know the way by road. There's a sort of cave behind a cove we landed at, and we went in there. Red met us. He came from his house on the cliff, he said, but I don't know how.'

Dick looked at Jo closely. 'I suppose you'll say next that there's a secret way from the cave to the house!' he said. 'Go on!'

'Must be,' said Jo. She suddenly glared at Dick. 'Don't you believe me? All right, find the place yourself!'

'Well – it does sound like a tale in a book,' said Julian. 'You're sure it *is* all true, Jo? We don't want to go on a wild-goose chase again, you know.'

'There's no wild goose in my story,' said Jo, puzzled. She hadn't the faintest idea what a wild-goose chase was. 'I'm telling you about Red. I'm ready to go when you are. We'll have to have a boat, though.'

'We'll take George's,' said Dick, getting up. 'Look, Jo – I think we'd better leave Anne behind this time. I don't like taking her into something that may be dangerous.'

'I want to come,' said Anne at once.

'No, you stay with me,' said Joan. 'I want company today. 'I'm getting scared of being by myself with all these things happening. You stay with me.'

So Anne stayed behind, really rather glad, and watched the other three go off together. Jo slipped into the hedge to avoid being seen by Jake, in case he was anywhere about. Julian and Dick went down to the beach and glanced round to make sure the gipsy was nowhere in sight.

They beckoned to Jo, and she came swiftly from hiding, and leapt into George's boat. She lay down in it so that she couldn't be seen. The boys hauled the boat down to the sea. Dick jumped in, and Julian pushed off when a big wave came. Then he jumped in too.

'How far up the coast is it?' he asked Jo, who was still at the bottom of the boat.

'I don't know,' said Jo, with her usual irritating vagueness. 'Two hours, three hours, maybe.'

Time didn't mean the same to Jo as it did to the others. For one thing Jo had no wrist-watch as they had, always there to be glanced at. She wouldn't have found one any use if she had, because she couldn't tell the time. Time was just day and night to her, nothing else.

Dick put up the little sail. The wind was in their favour, so he thought he might as well use it. They would get there all the more quickly.

'Did you bring the lunch that Joan put up for us?' said Julian to Dick. 'I can't see it anywhere.'

'Jo! You must be lying on it!' said Dick.

'It won't hurt it,' said Jo. She sat up as soon as they were well out to sea, and offered to take the tiller.

She was very deft with it, and the boys soon saw that they could leave her to guide the boat. Julian unfolded the map he had brought with him.

'I wonder whereabouts this place is where Red lives,' he said. 'It's pretty desolate all the way up to the next place, Port Limmersley. If there *is* a castle-like building, it must be a very lonely place to live in. There's not even a little fishing village shown for miles.'

The boat went on and on, scudding at times before a fairly strong wind. Julian took the tiller from Jo. 'We've come a long way already,' he said. 'Where *is* this place? Are you sure you'll know it, Jo?'

'Of course,' said Jo, scornfully. 'I think it's round that far-off rocky cliff.'

She was right. As they rounded the high cliff, which jutted fiercely with great slanting rocks, she pointed in triumph.

'There you are! See that place up there? That's Red's
place.'

The boys looked at it. It was a dour, grey stone building,
and was, as Jo had said, a little like a small castle. It
brooded over the sea, with one square tower overlooking
the waves.

'There's a cove before you come to the place,' said Jo. 'Watch out for it – it's very well hidden.'

It certainly was. The boat went right past it before they saw it. 'There it is!' cried Jo, urgently.

They took the sail down and then rowed back. The cove lay between two high layers of rock that jutted out from the cliff. They rowed right into it. It was very quiet and calm there, and their boat merely rose and fell as the water swelled and subsided under it.

'Can anyone see us from the house above?' asked Dick, as they rowed right to the back of the cove.

'I don't know,' said Jo. 'I shouldn't think so. Look – pull the boat up behind that big rock. We don't know who else might come here.'

They dragged the boat up. Dick draped it with great armfuls of seaweed, and soon it looked almost like a rock itself.

'Now, what next?' said Julian. 'Where's this cave you were talking about?'

'Up here,' said Jo, and began to climb up the rocky cliff like a monkey. Both the boys were very good climbers, but soon they found it impossible to get any further.

Jo scrambled down to them. 'What's the matter?' she said. 'If my Dad can climb up, surely you can!'

'Your Dad was an acrobat,' said Julian, sliding down a few feet, much too suddenly. 'Oooh! I don't much like this. I wish we had a rope.'

'There's one in the boat. I'll get it,' said Jo, and slithered down the cliff to the cove below at a most alarming rate. She climbed up again with the rope. She went on a good bit higher, and tied the rope to something. It hung down to where Dick and Julian stood clinging for dear life.

It was much easier to climb up with the help of a rope. Both boys were soon standing on a ledge, looking into a curious shaped cave. It was oval-shaped, and very dark.

'In here,' said Jo, and led the way. Dick and Julian followed stumblingly. Where in the world were they going to now?

Chapter Eighteen

THINGS BEGIN TO HAPPEN

Jo led them into a narrow rocky tunnel, and then out into a wider cave, whose walls dripped with damp. Julian was thankful for his torch. It was eerie and chilly and musty. He shivered. Something brushed his face and he leapt back.

'What was that?' he said.

'Bats,' said Jo, 'there's hundreds of them here. That's why the place smells so sour. Come on. We go round this rocky bit here into a better cave.'

They squeezed round a rocky corner and came into a drier cave that did not smell so strongly of bats. 'I haven't been any farther than this,' said Jo. 'This is where me and Dad came and waited for Red. He suddenly appeared, but I don't know where from.'

'Well, he must have come from somewhere,' said Dick, switching on his torch, too. 'There's a passage probably. We'll soon find it.'

He and Julian began to hunt round the cave, looking for a passage or little tunnel, or even a hole that led into the cliff, upwards towards the house. Obviously Red must have come down some such passage to reach the cave. Jo stayed in a corner, waiting. She had no torch.

Suddenly the boys had a tremendous shock. A voice boomed into their cave, a loud and angry voice that made their hearts beat painfully.

'SO! YOU DARE TO COME HERE!'

Jo slipped behind a rock immediately, like an animal going to cover. The boys stood where they were, rooted to the spot. Where did the voice come from?

'Who are you?' boomed the voice.

'Who are *you*?' shouted Julian. 'Come out and show yourself! We've come to see a man called Red. Take us to him.'

There was a moment's silence, as if the owner of the voice was rather taken aback. Then it boomed out again.

'Why do you want to see Red? Who sent you?'

'Nobody. We came because we want our cousin back, and her dog, too,' boomed Julian, making a funnel of his hands and trying to outdo the other voice.

There was another astonished silence. Then two legs appeared out of a hole in the low ceiling, and someone leapt lightly down beside them. The boys started back in surprise. They hadn't expected that the voice came from the roof of the cave!

Julian flashed his torch on the man. He was a giant-like fellow with flaming red hair. His eyebrows were red, too, and he had a red beard that partly hid a cruel mouth. Julian took one look into the man's eyes and then no more.

'He's mad,' he thought. 'So this is Red Tower. What is he? A scientist like Uncle Quentin, jealous of uncle's work? Or a thief working on a big scale, trying to get important papers and sell them? He's mad, whatever he is.'

Red was looking closely at the two boys. 'So you think I have your cousin,' he said. 'Who told you such a stupid tale?'

Julian didn't answer. Red took a threatening step towards him. 'Who told you?'

'I'll tell you that when the police come,' said Julian boldly.

Red stepped back.

'The police! What do they know? Why should they come here? Answer me, boy!'

'There's a lot to know about you, Mr. Red Tower,' said Julian. 'Who sent men to steal my uncle's papers? Who sent a note to ask for another lot? Who kidnapped our cousin, so that she could be held till the papers were sent? Who brought her here from Simmy's old caravan. Who...?'

'Aaaaaah!' said Red, and there was panic in his voice. 'How do you know all this? It isn't true! But the police – have they heard this fantastic tale, too?'

'What do you suppose?' said Julian, wishing with all his heart that the police *did* know, and that he was not merely bluffing. Red pulled at his beard. His green eyes gleamed as he thought quickly and urgently.

He suddenly called loudly, turning his head up to the hole in the ceiling. 'Markhoff! Come down!'

Two legs were swung down through the hole, and a short burly man leapt down beside the two startled boys.

'Go down the cliff. You will find a boat in the cove, somewhere – the boat we saw these boys coming in,' said Red sharply. 'Smash it to pieces. Then come back here and take the boys to the yard. Tie them up. We must leave quickly, and take the girl with us.'

The man stood listening, his face sullen. 'How can we go?' he said. 'You know the helicopter is not ready. You *know* that.'

'Make it ready then,' snapped Red. 'We leave tonight. The police will be here – do you hear that? This boy knows everything – he has told me – and the police must know everything too. I tell you, we must go.'

'What about the dog?' said the man.

'Shoot it,' ordered Red. 'Shoot it before we go. It's a brute of a dog. We should have shot it before. Now go and smash the boat.'

The man disappeared round the rocky corner that led into the cave of bats. Julian clenched his fist. He hated to think of George's boat being smashed to bits. Red stood there waiting, his eyes glinting in the light of the torches.

'I'd take you with us too, if there was room!' he suddenly snarled at Julian. 'Yes, and drop you into the sea!

'You can tell your uncle he'll hear from me about his precious daughter – we'll make an exchange. If he wants her back he can send me the notes I want. And many thanks for coming to warn me. I'll be off before the police break in.'

He began to pace up and down the cave, muttering. Dick and Julian watched in silence. They felt afraid for

George. Would Red really take her off in his helicopter? He looked mad enough for anything.

' The sullen man came back at last. 'It's smashed,' he said.

'Right,' said Red. 'I'll go first. Then the boys. Then you. And boot them if they make any trouble.'

Red swung himself up into the hole in the roof. Julian and Dick followed, not seeing any point in resisting. The man behind was too sulky to stand any nonsense. He followed immediately.

There had been no sign of Jo. She had kept herself well hidden, scared stiff. Julian didn't know what to do about her. He couldn't possibly tell Red about her – and yet it seemed terrible to leave her behind all alone. Well – she was a sharp-brained little monkey. Maybe she would think up something for herself.

Red led the way through another cave into a passage with such a low roof that he had to walk bent almost double.

The man behind had now switched on a very powerful torch, and it was easier to see. The passage sloped upwards and was obviously leading to the building on the cliff. At one part it was so steep that a hand-rail had been put for the climber to help himself up.

Then came a flight of steps hewn out of the rock itself – rough, badly-shaped steps, so steep that it was quite an effort to climb from one to the next.

At the top of the steps was a stout door set on a broad ledge. Red pushed it open and daylight flooded in. Julian blinked. He was looking out on an enormous yard

paved with great flat stones with weeds growing in all the
crevices and cracks.

In the middle stood a helicopter. It looked very strange
and out-of-place in that old yard. The house, with its
one tall square tower, was built round three sides of the
yard. It was covered with creeper and thick-stemmed ivy.

A high wall ran along the fourth side, with an enormous gate in the middle. It was shut, and from where he
stood Julian could see the huge bolts that were drawn
across.

'It's almost like a small fort,' thought Julian, in astonishment. Then he felt himself seized and taken to a shed nearby. His arms were forced behind him and his wrists were tightly tied. Then the rope was run through an iron loop and tied again.

Julian glared at the burly fellow now doing the same to Dick. He twisted about to try to see how the rope was tied, but he couldn't even turn, he was so tightly tethered.

He looked up at the tower. A small, forlorn face was looking out of the window there. Julian's heart jumped and beat fast. That must be poor old George up there. He wondered if she had seen them. He hoped not, because she would know that he and Dick had been captured, and she would be very upset.

Where was Timmy? There seemed no sign of him. But wait a minute – what was that lying inside what looked like a summer-house on the opposite side of the yard? *Was* it Timmy? Surely he would have barked a welcome when he heard them coming into the yard, if it *was* Timmy!

'Is that my cousin's dog?' he asked the sullen man.

The man nodded. 'Yes. He's been doped half the time, he barked so. Savage brute, isn't he? *Ought* to be shot, I reckon.'

Red had gone across the yard and had disappeared through a stone archway. The sullen man now followed him. Julian and Dick were left by themselves.

'We've muddled things again,' said Julian, with a groan. 'Now these fellows will be off and away, and take George with them – they've been nicely warned!'

Dick said nothing. He felt very miserable, and his bound wrists hurt him, too. Both boys stood there, wondering what would happen to them.

'Pssssssst!'

What was that? Julian turned round sharply and looked in the direction of the door that led from underground into the yard. Jo stood there, half-hidden by the archway over the door. 'Pssssst! I'll come and untie you. Is the coast clear?'

Chapter Nineteen

JO IS VERY SURPRISING

'Jo!' said the boys together, and their spirits lifted at once. 'Come on!'

There was no one about in the yard. Jo skipped lightly across from the doorway and slipped inside the shed.

'There's a knife in my back pocket,' said Julian. 'Get it out. It would be quicker to cut these ropes than to untie them. My word, Jo – I was never so pleased to see anyone in my life!'

Jo grinned as she hauled out Julian's sturdy pocket-knife. She opened it and ran her thumb lightly over the blade. It was beautifully sharp. She set to work to saw the blade across the thick rope. It cut easily through the fibres.

'I waited behind,' she said, rapidly. 'Then I followed when it was safe. But it was very dark and I didn't like it. Then I came to that door and peeped out. I was glad when I saw you.'

'Good thing the men didn't guess you were there,' said Dick. 'Good old Jo! I take back any nasty thing I've ever said about you!'

Jo beamed. She cut the last bit of rope that bound Julian, and he swung himself away from the iron loop

140

and began to rub his stiff, aching wrists. Jo set to work on Dick's bonds. She soon had those cut through, too.

'Where's George?' she asked, after she had helped Dick to rub his wrists and arms.

'Up in that tower,' said Julian. 'If we dared to go out in that yard you could look up and see her. And there's poor old Tim, look – half-doped – lying in that summer-house place over there.'

'I shan't let him be shot,' said Jo. 'He's a nice dog. I shall go and drag him down into those caves under-ground.'

'Not now!' said Julian, horrified. 'If you're seen now, you'll spoil everything. We'll *all* be tied up then!'

But Jo had already darted over to the summer-house and was fondling poor old Timmy.

The slam of a door made the boys jump and sent Jo into the shadows at the back of the summer-house at once. It was Red, coming across the yard!

'Quick! He's coming over here!' said Dick, in a panic. 'Let's get back to the iron loops and put our hands behind us so that he thinks we're still bound.'

So, when Red came over to the door of the shed, it looked exactly as if the boys still had their hands tied behind them. He laughed.

'You can stay here till the police come!' he said. Then he shut the shed door and locked it. He strolled over to the helicopter and examined it thoroughly. Then back he went to the door he had come from, opened it, and slammed it shut. He was gone.

When everything was quiet Jo sped back from the

summer-house to the shed. She unlocked the door of the shed. 'Come out,' she said. 'And we'll lock it again. Then nobody will know you aren't here. Hurry!'

There was nothing for it but to come out and hope there was nobody looking. Jo locked the shed door after them and hurried them back to the door that led underground. They slipped through it and half-fell down the steep steps.

'Thanks, Jo,' said Dick.

They sat down. Julian scratched his head, and for the life of him could not think of anything sensible to do. The police were *not* coming because they didn't know a thing about Red, or where George was or anything. And before long George would be flown off in that helicopter, and Timmy would be shot.

Julian thought of the high square tower and groaned. 'There's no way of getting George out of that tower,' he said aloud. 'It'll be locked and barred, or George would have got out at once. We can't even get to her. It's no good trying to make our way into the house – we'd be seen and caught at once.'

Jo looked at Dick. 'Do you badly want George to be rescued?' she said.

'That's a silly question,' said Dick. 'I want it more than anything else in the world.'

'Well – I'll go and get her, then,' said Jo, and she got up as if she really meant it.

'Don't make jokes now,' said Julian. 'This really is serious, Jo.'

'Well, so am I,' retorted Jo. 'I'll get her out, you see

if I don't. Then you'll know I'm trustable, won't you? You think I'm mean and thieving and not worth a ha'-penny, and I expect you're right. But I can do some things you can't, and if you want this thing, I'll do it for you.'

'How?' said Julian, astonished and disbelieving.

Jo sat down again.

'You saw that tower, didn't you?' she began. 'Well, it's a big one, so I reckon there's more than one room in it – and if I can get into the room next to George's I could undo her door and set her free.'

'And how do you think you're going to get into the room next to hers?' said Dick, scornfully.

'Climb up the wall, of course,' said Jo. 'It's set thick with ivy. I've often climbed up walls like that.'

The boys looked at her. 'Were you the Face at the Window by any chance?' said Julian, remembering Anne's fright. 'I bet you were. You're like a monkey, climbing and darting about. But you can't climb up that great high wall, so don't think it. You'd fall and be killed. We couldn't let you.'

'Pooh!' said Jo, with great scorn. 'Fall off a wall like that! I've climbed up a wall without any ivy at all! There's always holes and cracks to hold on to. That one would be easy!'

Julian was quite dumbfounded to think that Jo really meant all this. Dick remembered that Jo's father was an acrobat. Perhaps that kind of thing was in the family.

'You just ought to see me on a tight-rope,' said Jo earnestly. 'I can dance on it – and I never have a safety-net underneath – that's baby-play! Well, I'm going.'

Without another word she climbed
the steep steps lightly as a goat
and stood poised in the archway
of the door. All was quiet. Like
a squirrel she leapt and bounded
over the courtyard and came
to the foot of the ivy-covered
tower. Julian and Dick were now
at the doorway that led into the
yard, watching her.

'She'll be killed,' said Julian.

'Talk about pluck!' said Dick.
'I never saw such a kid in my life.
There she goes – just like a monkey.'

And, sure enough, up the ivy went
Jo, climbing lightly and steadily.
Her hands reached out and tested
each ivy-stem before she threw her
weight on it, and her feet tried
each one, too, before she stood on it.

Once she slipped when an ivy-stem came away from
the wall. Julian and Dick watched, their hearts in their
mouths. But Jo merely clutched at another piece of stem
and steadied herself once. Then up she went again.

Up and up. Past the first storey, past the second, and
up to the third. Only one more now and she would be
up to the topmost one. She seemed very small as she
neared the top.

'I can't bear to look and I can't bear not to,' said Dick,
pretending to shield his eyes and almost trembling with

nervousness. 'If she fell now – what should we do?'

'Do shut up,' said Julian, between his teeth. 'She won't fall. She's like a cat. There – she's making for the window next to George's. It's open at the bottom.'

Jo now sat triumphantly on the broad window-sill of the room next to George's. She waved impudently to the boys far below. Then she pushed with all her might at the window to open it a little more. It wouldn't budge.

So Jo laid herself flat, and by dint of much wriggling and squeezing, she managed to slip through the narrow space between the bottom of the window-pane and the sill. She disappeared from sight.

Both boys heaved heartfelt sighs of relief. Dick found that his knees were shaking. He and Julian retired into the underground passage below the steep steps and sat there in silence.

'Worse than a circus,' said Dick at last. 'I'll never be able to watch acrobats again. What's she doing now, do you suppose?'

Jo was very busy. She had fallen off the inside window-sill with a bump, and bruised herself on the floor below. But she was used to bruises.

She picked herself up and shot behind a chair in case anyone had heard her. Nobody seemed to have heard anything, so she peeped cautiously out. The room was furnished with enormous pieces of furniture, old and heavy. Dust was on everything, and cobwebs hung down from the stone ceiling.

Jo tiptoed to the door. Her feet were bare and made no sound at all. She looked out. There was a spiral stone stairway nearby going downwards, and on each side was a door – there must be four rooms in the tower then, one for each corner, two windows in each. She looked at the door next to the room she was in. That must be the door of George's room.

There was a very large key in the lock, and a great bolt had been drawn across. Jo leapt across and dragged at the bolt. It made a loud noise and she darted back into the room again. But still nobody came. Back she went to the door again, and this time turned the enormous key. It was well oiled and turned easily.

Jo pushed open the door and put her head cautiously round. George was there – a thin and unhappy George, sitting by the window. She stared at Jo as if she couldn't believe her eyes!

'Psssst!' said Jo, enjoying all this very much indeed. 'I've come to get you out!'

Chapter Twenty

THE ADVENTURE BOILS UP

GEORGE looked as if she had seen a ghost. '**Jo!**' she whispered. 'It can't really be you.'

'It is. Feel,' said Jo, and pattered across the room to give George quite a hard pinch. Then she pulled at her arm.

'Come on,' she said. 'We must go before Red comes. Hurry! I don't want to be caught.'

George got up as if she was in a dream. She went across to the door. She and Jo slipped out, and stood at the top of the spiral staircase.

'Have to go down here, I suppose,' said Jo. She cocked her head and listened. Then she went down a few steps and turned the first spiral bend.

But before she had gone down more than a dozen steps she stopped in fright. Somebody was coming up!

In panic Jo ran up again and pushed George roughly into the room she had climbed into first of all.

'Someone's coming,' she panted. 'Now we're finished.'

'It's that red-haired man, I expect,' said George. 'He

comes up three or four times a day and tries to make me tell him about my father's work. But I don't know a thing. What are we to do?'

The slow steps came up and up, sounding hollowly on the stone stairs. They could hear a panting breath now, too.

An idea came to Jo. She put her mouth close to George's ear. 'Listen! We look awfully alike. I'll let myself be caught and locked up in that room – and you take the chance to slip down and go to Dick and Julian. Red will never know I'm not you – we've even got the same clothes on now, because Joan gave me old ones of yours.'

'No,' said George, astounded. 'You'll be caught. I don't want you to do that.'

'You've *got* to,' whispered Jo, fiercely. 'Don't be daft. I can open the window and climb down the ivy, easy as winking, when Red's gone. It's your only chance. They're going to take you off in that helicopter tonight.'

The footsteps were now at the top. Jo pushed George well behind a curtain and whispered fiercely again: 'Anyway, I'm not really doing this for you. I'm doing it for Dick. You keep there and I'll do the rest.'

There was a loud exclamation when the man outside discovered the door of George's room open. He went in quickly and found nobody there. Out he came and yelled down the stairs.

'Markhoff! The door's open and the girl's gone! Who opened the door?'

Markhoff came up two steps at a time, looking bewildered. 'No one! Who could? Anyway, the girl can't be far off! I've been in the room below all the time since I locked her in last time. I'd have seen her if she's gone.'

'Who unlocked the door?' screamed Red, quite beside himself with anger. 'We've *got* to have that girl to bargain with.'

'Well, she must be in one of the other rooms,' said Markhoff, stolidly, quite unmoved by his master's fury. He went into one on the opposite side to the room where Jo and George crouched trembling. Then he came into their room, and at once saw the top of Jo's head showing behind the chair.

He pounced on her and dragged her out. 'Here she is!' he said, and didn't seem to realize that it was not George at all, but Jo. With their short hair, freckled faces and their similar clothes they really were alike. Jo yelled and struggled most realistically. Nobody would have guessed that she had planned to be caught and locked up!

George shook and shivered behind the curtain, longing to go to Jo's help, but knowing that it wouldn't be of the least use. Besides – there might be a chance now of finding Timmy. It had almost broken George's heart to be parted from him for so long.

Jo was dragged yelling and kicking into the room and locked in again. Red and Markhoff began to quarrel about which of them must have left the door unlocked.

'You were there last,' said Red.

'Well, if I was, I tell you I didn't leave the door unlocked,' Markhoff raged back. 'I wouldn't be so fatheaded. That's the kind of thing *you* do.'

'That'll do,' snapped Red. 'Have you shot that dog

yet? No, you haven't! Go down and do it before *he* es-
capes too!'

George's heart went stone-cold. Shoot Timmy! Oh
no! Dear darling old Timmy. She couldn't let him be
shot!

She didn't know what to do. She heard Red and
Markhoff go down the stone stairway, their boots making
a terrific noise at first, and then gradually becoming
fainter.

She slipped down after them. They went into a nearby
room, still arguing. George risked being seen and shot
past the open door. She came to another stairway, not a
spiral one this time, and went down it so fast that she
almost lost her footing. Down and down and down. She
met nobody at all. What a very strange place this was!

She came into a dark, enormous hall that smelt musty
and old. She ran to the great door at the front and tried
to open it. It was very heavy, but at last it swung slowly
back.

She stood there in the bright sunlight, peering out
cautiously. She knew where Timmy was. She had been
able to see him sometimes, flopping queerly in and out of
the summer-house. She knew that because of his continual
barking he had been doped. Red had told her that when
she had asked him. He enjoyed making her miserable.
Poor George!

She tore across the courtyard and came to the summer-
house. Timmy was there, lying as if he were asleep.
George flung herself on him, her arms round his thick
neck.

'Timmy, oh Timmy!' she cried, and couldn't see him for tears. Timmy, far away in some drugged dream, heard the voice he loved best in all the world. He stirred. He opened his eyes and saw George!

He was too heavy with his sleep to do more than lick her face. Then his eyes closed again. George was in despair. She was afraid Markhoff would come and shoot him in a very short time.

'Timmy!' she called in his ear. 'TIMMY! Do wake up. TIMMY!'

Tim opened his eyes again. What – his mistress still here! Then it couldn't be a dream. Perhaps his world would soon be right again. Timmy didn't understand at all what had been happening the last few days. He staggered to his feet somehow and stood swaying there, shaking his head. George put her hand on his collar. 'That's right, Tim,' she said. 'Now you come with me. Quick!'

But Timmy couldn't walk, though he had managed to stand. In despair George glanced over the courtyard, fearful that she would see Markhoff coming at any moment.

She saw somebody else. She saw Julian standing in an archway opposite, staring at her. She was too upset about Timmy even to feel much astonishment.

'Ju!' she called. 'Come and help me with Timmy. They're going to shoot him!'

In a trice Julian and Dick shot across the courtyard to George. 'What happened, Jo?' said Julian. 'Did you find George?'

'Ju – it's me, George!' said George, and Julian suddenly saw that indeed it was George herself. He had been so certain that it was still Jo that he hadn't known it was George!

'Help me with Timmy,' said George, and she pulled at the heavy dog. 'Where shall we hide him?'

'Down underground,' said Dick. 'It's the only place. Come on!'

How they managed it they never quite knew, but they did drag the heavy, stupid Timmy all the way across the yard and into the archway. They opened the door and shoved him inside. Poor Timmy fell over and immediately rolled down the steep steps, landing at the bottom with a frightful thud. George gave a little scream.

'He'll be hurt!'

But astonishingly enough Timmy didn't seem to be hurt at all. In fact the shaking seemed to have done him good. He got up and looked round him in rather a surprised way. Then he whined and looked up at George. He tried to climb the steep steps, but wasn't lively enough.

George was down beside him in a moment, patting him and stroking him. The two boys joined in. Timmy began to feel that things might be all right again, if only he could get rid of the dreadful, heavy feeling in his head. He couldn't understand why he kept wanting to lie down and go to sleep.

'Bring him right down to the caves,' said Dick. 'Those men are sure to hunt for him and for us too when they find Timmy gone, and us not in the shed.'

So down the narrow passages and into the little cave

with the hole in the roof they all went, Timmy feeling as if he didn't quite know which of his legs to use next.

They all sat down in a heap together when they got there, and George got as close to Timmy as she could. She was glad when the boys switched off their torches. She badly wanted to cry, and as she never did cry it was most embarrassing if anyone saw her.

She told the boys in a low voice all that had happened with Jo. 'She *made* me stay hidden so that she could be caught,' she said. 'She's wonderful. She's the bravest girl I ever knew. And she did it all even though she doesn't like me.'

'She's a queer one,' said Dick. 'She's all right at heart, though – very much all right.'

They talked quickly, in low voices, exchanging their news. George told them how she had been caught and taken to the caravan with Timmy, who had been knocked out with a cudgel.

'We saw where you had written Red's name,' said Dick. 'That gave us the clue to come here!'

'Listen,' said Julian, suddenly. 'I think we ought to make a plan quickly. I keep thinking I hear things. We're sure to be looked for soon, you know. What can we *do*?'

Chapter Twenty-One

A FEW SURPRISES

As soon as Julian had said that he kept hearing noises, the others felt as if they could hear some, too. They sat and listened intently, George's heart beating so loudly that she was certain the boys would be able to hear it.

'I think perhaps it's the sound of the sea, echoing in through the caves and the tunnels,' said Julian at last. 'In the ordinary way, of course, we wouldn't need to bother to listen – Timmy would growl at once! But, poor old chap, he's so doped and sleepy that I don't believe he hears anything.'

'Will he get all right again?' asked George, anxiously, fondling Timmy's silky ears.

'Oh, yes,' said Julian, sounding much more certain than he really felt. Poor Timmy – he really did seem ill! There wasn't even a growl in him.

'You've had an awful time these last few days, haven't you George?' asked Dick.

'Yes,' said George. 'I don't much want to talk about it. If I'd had Timmy with me it wouldn't have been so bad, but at first, when they brought me here, all I knew of Timmy was hearing him bark and snarl and bark and snarl down below in that yard. Then Red told me he had doped him.'

'How did you get to Red's place?' asked Julian.

'Well, you know I was locked in that horrible-smelling caravan,' said George. 'Then suddenly a man called Simmy – he's Jo's father, I think – came and dragged us out. Timmy was all stupid with the blow they'd given him – and they put him in a sack and put us both on the caravan horse and took us through the wood and along a desolate path by the coast till we came here. That was in the middle of the night.'

'Poor old George!' said Julian. 'I wish Tim was himself again – I'd love to set him loose on Red and the other fellow!'

'I wonder what's happening to Jo,' said Dick, suddenly remembering that Jo was now imprisoned in the tower room where George had been kept so long.

'And do you suppose Red and Markhoff have discovered that we've got out of that shed, and that Timmy has disappeared, too?' said Julian. 'They'll be in a fury when they do discover it!'

'Can't we get away?' said George, feeling suddenly scared. 'You came in a boat, didn't you? Well, can't we get away in that and go and fetch help for Jo?'

There was a silence. Neither of the boys liked to tell George that her beloved boat had been smashed to pieces by Markhoff. But she had to know, of course, and Julian told her in a few short words.

George said nothing at all. They all sat silently for a few minutes, hearing nothing but Timmy's heavy, almost snoring, breathing.

'Would it be possible, when it's dark, to creep up into the courtyard, and go round the walls to the big gate?'

said Dick, breaking the silence. 'We can't escape any-where down here, it's certain – not without a boat, anyhow.'

'Should we wait till Red and Markhoff have gone off in the helicopter?' said Julian. 'Then we'd be much safer.'

'Yes – but what about Jo?' asked Dick. 'They think she's George, don't they? – and they'll take her away with them, just as they planned to do with George. I don't see how we can try to escape ourselves without first trying to save Jo. She's been a brick about George.'

They talked round and round the idea of trying to save Jo, but nobody could think of any really sensible plan at all. Time went on, and they all felt hungry and rather cold. 'If only we could *do* something, it wouldn't be so bad!' groaned Dick. 'I wonder what's happening up at the house.'

Up at the grey stone house with its big square-tower, plenty was happening!

To begin with, Markhoff had gone to shoot Timmy, as Red had ordered. But when he got to the summer-house there was no dog there!

Markhoff stared in the greatest amazement! The dog had been tied up, even though he was doped – and now, there was the loose rope, and no dog attached to it!

Markhoff gazed round the summer-house in astonish-ment. Who could have loosed Timmy? He darted across to the locked shed where he had tied Julian and Dick with rope to the iron staples. The door was still locked, of course – and Markhoff turned the key and pushed it open.

'Here, you . . .' he began, shouting roughly. Then he stopped dead. Nobody was there! Again there was loose rope – this time cut here and there, so that it lay in short pieces – and again the prisoners had gone. No dog. No boys.

Markhoff couldn't believe his eyes. He looked all round the shed. 'But it was locked from the outside!' he muttered. 'What's all this? Who's freed the dog and the boys? What will Red say?'

Markhoff looked at the helicopter standing ready for flight in the middle of the yard, and half decided to desert Red and get away himself. Then, remembering Red's mad tempers, and his cruel revenges on anyone who dared to let him down, he changed his mind.

'We'd better get off now, before it's dark,' he thought. 'There's something queer going on here. There must be somebody else here that we know nothing about. I'd better find Red and tell him.'

He went in through the massive front door, and in the hall he came face to face with two men waiting there. At first he couldn't see who they were, and he stepped back hurriedly. Then he saw it was Simmy and Jake.

'What are you doing here?' shouted Markhoff. 'Weren't you told to keep watch on Kirrin Cottage and make sure the police weren't told anything?'

'Yes,' said Jake, sulkily. 'And we've come to say that that cook – woman called Joan – went down to the police this morning. She had one of the kids with her – a girl. The boys don't seem to be about.'

'No. They're here – at least, they were,' said Markhoff. 'They've disappeared again. As for the police, we've heard they're on the way, and we've made our plans. You're a bit late with your news! Lot of good you are, with your spying! Clear off now – we're taking the girl off in the helicopter before the police come. How did any-one know where the girl was? Have you been spilling the beans?'

'Pah!' said Simmy, contemptuously. 'Think we want to be messed up with the police? You must be mad. We want some money. We've done all your dirty work, and you've only paid us half you promised. Give us the rest.'

'You can ask Red for it!' growled Markhoff. 'What's the good of asking me? Go and ask *him*!'

'Right. We will,' said Jake, his face as black as thunder. 'We've done all he told us – took the papers for him, took the girl – and that savage brute of a dog too – see where he bit me on my hand? And all we get is half our money! I reckon we've only just come in time, too. Planning to go off in that there heli-thing and do us out of our pay. Pah!'

'Where's Red?' demanded Simmy.

'Upstairs,' said Markhoff. 'I've got some bad news for him, so he won't be pleased to see you and your ugly mugs. Better let me find him for you and say what I've got to say – then you can chip in with your polite little speeches.'

'Funny, aren't you?' said Jake, in a dangerous voice. Neither he nor Simmy liked Markhoff. They followed him up the broad stairway, and then up again till they came to the room that lay below the spiral staircase.

Red was there, scanning through the papers that had been stolen from the study of George's father. He was in a black temper. He flung down the papers as Markhoff came in.

'These aren't the notes I wanted!' he began, loudly. 'Well, I'll hold the girl till I get . . . why, Markhoff, what's up? Anything wrong?'

'Plenty,' said Markhoff. 'The dog's gone – he wasn't there when I went to shoot him – and the two boys have gone too – yes, escaped out of a locked shed. Beats me!

'And here are two visitors for you – they want money! They've come to tell you what you already know – the police have been told about you.'

Red went purple in the face, and his strange eyes shone with rage. He stared first at Markhoff, then at Simmy and Jake. Markhoff looked uneasy, but Simmy and Jake looked back insolently.

'You – you – you *dare* to come here when I told you to keep away!' he shouted. 'You've BEEN paid. You can't blackmail me for any more money.'

What he would have said next nobody knew because from up the spiral stairs there came yells and screams and the noise of someone apparently trying to batter down a door.

'That's that girl, I suppose,' muttered Markhoff. 'What's up with her? She's been quiet enough before.'

'We'd better get her out now and go,' said Red, his face still purple. 'Jake, go and get her. Bring her down here, and knock some sense into her if she goes on screaming.'

'Fetch her yourself,' said Jake, insolently.

Red looked at Markhoff, who immediately produced a revolver.

'My orders are always obeyed,' said Red in a suddenly cold voice. '*Always*, you understand?'

Not only Jake scuttled up the stairs then but also Simmy! They went to the locked and bolted room at the top and unlocked the door. They pulled back the bolt and door. Simmy stepped into the room to deal with the imprisoned girl.

But he stopped dead and gaped. He blinked, rubbed his eyes and gaped again. Jake gaped too.

'Hallo, Dad!' said Jo. 'You *do* seem surprised to see me!'

Chapter Twenty-Two

JO IS VERY SMART

'Jo' said Simmy. 'Well, of all the . . . well . . . *JO*!' Jake recovered first. 'What's all this?' he said, roughly, to Simmy. 'What's Jo doing here? How did *she* get here? Where's the other kid, the one we caught?'

'How do *I* know?' said Simmy, still staring at Jo. 'Look here, Jo – what are you doing here? Go on, tell us. And where's the other kid?'

'Hunt round the room and see if you can find her!' said Jo, brightly, keeping on her toes in case her father or Jake was going to pounce on her. The two men looked hurriedly round the room. Jake went to a big cupboard.

'Yes – she might be in there,' said Jo, enjoying herself. 'You have a good look.'

The two bewildered men didn't know what to think. They had come to get George – and had only found Jo!

But how – why – what had happened? They didn't know what to do. Neither of them wanted to go back and tell Red. So they began to search the room feverishly, looking into likely and unlikely places, with Jo jeering at them all the time.

'Better take the drawers out of that chest and see if

she's here. And don't forget to look under the rug.
That's right, Jake, poke your head up the chimney. Mind
George doesn't kick soot down into your eyes.'

'I'll lam you in a minute!' growled Jake, furiously,
opening a small cupboard door.

An angry voice came up the stairway. 'Jake! What
are you doing up there? Bring that kid down.'

'She's not here!' yelled back Jake, suddenly losing
his temper. 'What have you done with her? She's gone!'

Red came tearing up, two steps at a time, his eyes narrow with anger. The first thing he saw in the room was
Jo – and, of course, he thought she was George.

'What do you mean – saying she's not here!' he raged.
'Are you mad?'

'Nope,' said Jake, his eyes narrow too. 'Not so mad as
you are, anyway, Red. This kid isn't that fellow's daughter – the scientist chap we took the papers from – this is
Simmy's kid – Jo.'

Red looked at Jake as if he had gone off his head. Then
he looked at Jo. He could see no difference between Jo
and the absent George at all – short hair, freckles, turned-
up nose – he couldn't believe that she was Simmy's
daughter.

In fact, he didn't believe it. He thought Jake and
Simmy were suddenly deceiving him for some strange
reason.

But Jo had a word to say, too. 'Yes, I'm Jo,' she said.
'I'm not Georgina. She's gone. I'm just Jo, and Simmy's
my Dad. You've come to save me, haven't you, Dad?'

Simmy hadn't come to do anything of the sort, of

course. He stared helplessly at Jo, completely bewildered.

Red completely lost his temper. As soon as he heard Jo's voice he realized she was not George. Somehow or other he had been deceived – and seeing that this was Simmy's daughter, then it must be Simmy who had had a hand in the deception!

He went suddenly over to Simmy and struck him hard, his eyes blazing. 'Have you double-crossed me?' he shouted.

Simmy was sent flying to the floor. Jake came up immediately to help him. He tripped up Red, and leapt on him.

Jo looked at the three struggling, shouting men, and shrugged her shoulders. Let them fight! They had forgotten all about her, and that suited her very well. She ran to the door and was just going down the stairs, when an idea came into her sharp little mind. With an impish grin she turned back. She pulled the door to quietly – and then she turned the key in the lock, and shot the bolt.

The three men inside heard the key turn, and in a trice Jake was at the door, pulling at the handle.

'She's locked us in!' he raged. 'And shot the bolt, too.'

'Yell for Markhoff!' shouted Red, trembling with fury. And Markhoff, left down in the room at the bottom of the stairs, suddenly heard yells and shouts and tremendous hammerings at the door! He tore up at once, wondering what in the world had happened.

Jo was hiding in the next room. As soon as Markhoff went to the door and shot back the bolt she slipped out and was down the spiral stairway in a trice, unseen by Markhoff. She grinned to herself and hugged something to her thin little chest.

It was the big key belonging to the door upstairs. Nobody could unlock that door now – the key was missing. Jo had it!

'Unlock the door!' shouted Red. 'That kid's gone.'

'There's no key!' yelled back Markhoff. 'She must have taken it. I'll go after her.'

But it was one thing to go after Jo and quite another to find her. She seemed to have disappeared into thin air.

Markhoff raged through every room, but she was nowhere to be seen. He went out into the courtyard and looked round there.

Actually she had made her way to the kitchen and found the larder. She was very hungry and wanted something to eat. There was nobody in the kitchen at all, though a fine fire burned in the big range there.

She slipped into the larder, took the key from the outer side of the door and locked herself in. She saw that there was a small window, and she carefully unfastened it so that she could make her escape if anyone discovered that she was locked in the larder.

Then she tucked in. Three sausage rolls, a large piece of cheese, a hunk of bread, half a meat pie and two jam tarts went the same way. After that Jo felt a lot better. She remembered the others and thought how hungry they must be feeling, too.

She found a rush bag hanging on a nail and slipped some food into it – more sausage rolls, some rock-buns, some cheese and bread. Now, if only she could find the others, how they would welcome her!

Jo put the big key at the bottom of the rush basket. She was feeling very, very pleased with herself. Red and Simmy and Jake were all nicely locked up and out of the way. She didn't fear Markhoff as much as Red. She was sure she could get away from him.

She wasn't even sorry for her father, Simmy.

She had no love for him and no respect, because he was everything that a father shouldn't be.

She heard Markhoff come raging into the kitchen and she clambered quickly up on the larder shelf, ready to drop out of the window if he tried the door. But he didn't. He raged out again, and she heard him no more.

Jo unlocked the door very cautiously. There was now an old woman in the kitchen, standing by the table, folding some clothes she had brought in from the clothes line in the yard. She stared in the greatest surprise at Jo peeping out of the larder.

'What . . .?' she began, indignantly; but Jo was out of the room before she had even got out the next word. The old dame waddled over to the larder and began to wail as she saw all the empty plates and dishes.

Jo went cautiously into the front hall. She could hear Markhoff upstairs, still tearing about. She smiled delightedly and slipped over to the door.

She undid it and pulled it open. Then, keeping to the wall, she sidled like a weasel to the door that led underground. She opened it and went through, shutting it softly behind her.

Now to find the others. She felt sure they must be down in the caves. How pleased they would be with the food in her bag!

She half-fell down the steep steps, and made her way as quickly as she could down the slanting passage. She had no torch and had to feel her way in the dark. She wasn't in the least afraid. Only when she trod on a sharp stone with her bare foot did she make a sound.

The other three – Julian, Dick and George – were still sitting crouched together with Timmy in the centre. Julian had been once up to the door that led into the yard and had cautiously peered out to see what was to be seen – but had seen nothing at all except for an old woman hanging out some clothes on a line.

The three had decided to wait till night before they did anything. They thought maybe Timmy might have recovered a little then, and would be of some help in protecting them against Red or Markhoff. They half-dozed, sitting together for warmth, enjoying the heat of Timmy's big body.

Timmy growled! Yes, he actually growled – a thing he hadn't done at all so far. George put a warning hand on him. They all sat up, listening. A voice came to them.

'Julian! Dick! Where are you? I've lost my way!'

'It's Jo!' cried Dick, and switched on his torch at once. 'Here we are, Jo! How did you escape? What's happened?'

'Heaps,' said Jo, and came gladly over to them. 'My, it was dark up in those passages without a torch. Somehow I went the wrong way. That's why I yelled. But I hadn't gone far wrong. Have a sausage roll?'

'*What?*' cried three hungry voices, and even Timmy lifted his head and began to sniff at the rush basket that Jo carried.

Jo laughed and opened the basket. She handed out all the food and the three of them fell on it like wolves. 'Jo, you're the eighth wonder of the world,' said Dick. 'Is there anything left in the basket?'

'Yes,' said Jo, and took out the enormous key. 'This, look! I locked Red and Jake and Simmy into that tower room, and here's the key. What do you think of *that*?'

Chapter Twenty-Three

MARKHOFF GOES HUNTING

GEORGE took the big key and looked at it with awe. 'Jo! Is this really the key – and you've locked them all in? Honestly, I think you're a marvel.'

'She is,' said Dick, and to Jo's enormous delight he gave her a sudden quick hug. 'I never knew such a girl in my life. Never. She's got the pluck of twenty!'

'It was easy, really,' said Jo, her eyes shining joyfully in the light of the torch. 'You trust me now, Dick, don't you? You won't be mean to me any more, any of you, will you?'

'Of course not,' said Julian. 'You're our friend for ever!'

'Not George's,' said Jo at once.

'Oh yes you are,' said George. 'I take back every single mean thing I said about you. You're as good as a boy.'

This was the very highest compliment that George could ever pay any girl. Jo beamed and gave George a light punch.

'I did it all for Dick, really,' she said. 'But next time I'll do it for you!'

'Goodness, I hope there won't *be* a next time,' said

George, with a shiver. 'I can't say I enjoyed one single minute of the last few days.'

Timmy suddenly put his head on Jo's knee. She stroked him. 'Look at that!' she said. 'He remembers me. He's better, isn't he, George?'

George carefully removed Timmy's head from Jo's knee to her own. She felt decidedly friendly towards Jo now, but not to the extent of having Timmy put his head on Jo's knee. She patted him.

'Yes, he's better,' she said. 'He ate half the sausage roll I gave him, though he sniffed at it like anything first. I think he knows something has been put into his food and now he's suspicious of it. Good old Timmy.'

They all felt much more lively and cheerful now that they were no longer so dreadfully empty. Julian looked at his watch. 'It's getting on towards evening now,' he said. 'I wonder what all those fellows are doing.'

Three of them were still locked up! No matter how Markhoff had tried to batter in the door, it held. It was old and immensely strong, and the lock held without showing any sign of giving way even an eighth of an inch. Two other men had been called in from the garage to help, but except that the door looked decidedly worse for wear, it stood there just the same, sturdy and unbreakable.

Simmy and Jake watched Red as he walked up and down the tower room like a caged lion. They were glad they were two against one. He seemed like a madman to them as he raged and paced up and down.

Markhoff, outside with the other two men he had

brought up to help, was getting very worried. No police had arrived as yet (and wouldn't either, because Joan hadn't been able to tell them anything except that she knew Julian and Dick had gone to see a man called Red – but where he lived she had no idea!).

But Red and Markhoff didn't know this – they felt sure that a police ambush was somewhere nearby. If only they could get away in the helicopter before anything else happened!

'Markhoff! Take Carl and Tom and go down into those underground caves,' ordered Red at last. 'Those children are sure to be there – it's the only place for them to hide. They can't get out of here because the front gate is locked and bolted, and the wall's too high to climb. Get hold of the kids and search them for the key.'

So Markhoff and two burly fellows went downstairs and out of the door. They crossed the yard to the door that led to the caves.

They got down the steep steps and were soon stumbling along the narrow, slanting passage, their nailed boots making a great noise as they went. They hung on to the hand-rail when they came to the difficult stretch of tunnel, and finally came out into the cave that had the hole in the floor.

There was nobody there. The children had heard the noise of the coming men, and had hurriedly swung themselves down through the hole into the cave below.

They ran through into another cave, the sour smelling one where bats lived and slept. Then round the rocky corner into the first cave, the curious oval-shaped one that led out to the ledge of rock overlooking the steep cliff.

'There's nowhere to hide,' groaned Julian. He looked back into the cave. At least it was better in there than out on this ledge, outlined by the daylight. He pulled the others back into the cave, and shone his torch up and down the walls to find some corner that they could squeeze behind.

Half-way up the wall was a shelf of rock. He hoisted George up there, and she dragged Timmy up too. Poor Timmy – he wasn't much use to them; he was still so bemused and so very sleepy. He had growled at the noise made by the coming men, but had dropped his head again almost immediately.

Dick got up beside George. Julian found a jutting-out rock and tried to hide behind it, while Jo lay down in a hole beside one wall and covered herself cleverly with sand. Julian couldn't help thinking how sharp Jo was. She always seemed to know the best thing to do.

But as it happened, Jo was the only one to be discovered! It was quite by accident – Markhoff trod on her. He and the other two men had let themselves down through the hole into the cave below, had then gone into the cave of bats, seen no sign of anyone there, and were now in the cave that led to the cliff.

'Those kids aren't here,' said one of the men. 'They've gone to hide somewhere else. What a horrible place this is – let's go back.'

Markhoff was flashing his torch up and down the walls to see if any of the children were crouching behind a jutting rock – and he trod heavily on Jo's hand. She gave an agonized yell, and Markhoff almost dropped his torch!

In a trice he had pulled the girl out of her bed of sand and was shaking her like a rat. 'This is the one we want!' he said to the others. 'She's got the key. Where is it, you little rat? Give it to me or I'll throw you down the cliff!'

Julian was horrified. He felt quite certain that Markhoff really would throw Jo down the cliff, and he was just about to jump down to help her, when he heard her speak.

'All right. Let me go, you brute. Here's the key! You go and let my Dad out before the police come! I don't want him caught!'

Markhoff gave an exclamation of triumph, and snatched a shining key out of Jo's hand. He gave her a resounding box on the ear.

'You little toad! You can just stay down here with the others, and it'll be a very, very long stay! Do you know what we're going to do? We're going to roll a big rock over the hole in that other cave's roof – and you'll be prisoners!

'You can't escape upwards – and you won't be able to escape downwards. You'll be dashed on the rocks by the sea if you try to swim away. That'll teach you to interfere!'

The other two men guffawed. 'Good idea Mark,' said one. 'They'll all be nicely boxed up here and nobody will know where they are! Come on – we've no time to lose. If Red isn't unlocked soon he'll go mad!'

They made their way into the heart of the cliff again, and the listening children heard their footsteps getting fainter. Finally they ceased altogether, as one by one the men levered themselves up through the hole in the roof of the last cave, and disappeared up the narrow, low-roofed tunnel that led to the courtyard.

Julian came out from his hiding-place, looking grim and rather scared. 'That's done it!' he said. 'If those fellows really do block up that hole – and I bet they have already – it looks as if we're here for keeps! As he said, we can't get up, and we can't escape down – the sea's too rough for us to attempt any swimming, and the cliff's unclimbable above the ledge!'

'I'll go and have a look and see if they *have* blocked up that hole,' said Dick. 'They may be bluffing.'

But it hadn't been bluff. When Julian and Dick shone their torches on to the hole in the roof, they saw that a great rock was now blocking it up.

They could not get through the hole again. It was impossible to move the rock from below. They went soberly back to the front cave and sat out on the ledge in the light of the sinking sun.

'It's a pity poor Jo was found,' said George. 'And an even greater pity she had to give up the key! Now Red and the others will go free.'

'They won't,' said Jo, surprisingly. 'I didn't give them the key of the tower room. I'd another key with me – the key of the kitchen larder! And I gave them that.'

'Well, I'm blessed!' said Julian, astounded. 'The things

you do, Jo! But how on earth did you happen to have the key of the *larder*?'

Jo told them how she had taken it out and locked herself in when she was having a meal there.

'I had to unlock the door to get out again, of course,' she said. 'And I thought I'd take that key, too, because, who knows? – I might have wanted to get into that larder again and lock myself in with the food!'

'No one will ever get the better of you, Jo,' said Dick with the utmost conviction. 'Never. You're as cute as a bagful of monkeys. So you've still got the right key with you?'

'Yes,' said Jo. 'And Red and my Dad and Jake are still locked up in the tower room!'

But suddenly a most disagreeable thought struck Dick. 'Wait a bit!' he said. 'What's going to happen when they find they've got the *wrong* key? They'll be down here again, and my word, what'll happen to us all then!'

Chapter Twenty-Four

A GRAND SURPRISE

THE thought that the men might soon return even angrier than they had been before was most unpleasant.

'As soon as Markhoff tries the key in the door of the tower room he'll find it won't unlock it, and he'll know that Jo has tricked him!' said George.

'And then he'll be in such a fury that he'll tear down here again, and goodness knows what will happen to us!' groaned Julian. 'What shall we do? Hide again?'

'No,' said Dick. 'Let's get out of here and climb down the cliff to the sea. I'd feel safer there than up here in this cave. We might be able to find a better hiding-place down on the rocks in that little cove.'

'It's a pity my boat's smashed,' said George, with a sigh for her lovely boat. 'And, I say – how are we going to get old Timmy down?'

There was a conference about this. Timmy couldn't climb down, that was certain. Jo remembered the rope still hanging down the side of the cliff to the ledges below – the one she had tied there to help Julian and Dick climb up the steep sides of the cliff.

'I know,' she said, her quick mind working hard again. 'You go down first, Julian, then Dick. Then

George can go – each of you holding on to the rope as you climb down, in case you fall.

'Then I'll haul up the rope and tie old Timmy to it, round his waist – and I'll lower him down to you. He's so sleepy still, he won't struggle. He won't even know what's happening!'

'But what about you?' said Dick. 'You'll be last of all. Will you mind? You'll be all alone up on this ledge, with the men coming behind you at any minute.'

'No, I don't mind,' said Jo. 'But let's be quick.'

Julian went down first, glad of the rope to hold to as his feet and hands searched for crevices and cracks. Then came Dick, almost slipping in his anxiety to get down.

Then George climbed down, slowly and anxiously, not at all liking the steep cliff. Once she glanced down to the sea below, and felt sick. She shut her eyes for a moment and clung with one hand to the rope.

It was a dreadful business getting Timmy down. George stood below, anxiously waiting. Jo found it very difficult to tie Timmy safely. He was big and heavy, and didn't like being tied up at all, though he really seemed hardly to know what was going on. At last Jo had got the knots well and securely tied, and called out to the others.

'Here he comes. Watch out that the rope doesn't break. Oh, dear – I wish he wouldn't struggle – now he's bumped himself against the cliff!'

It was not at all a nice experience for poor Timmy. He swung to and fro on the rope as he was slowly let down, and was amazed to find that he was suspended in mid air. Above him Jo panted and puffed.

'Oh, he's so awfully heavy! I hope I shan't have to let go. Look out for him!' she screamed.

The weight was too much for her just at the last, and the rope was let out with rather a rush. Fortunately Timmy was only about six feet up then, and Julian and George managed to catch him as he suddenly descended.

'I'm coming now,' called Jo, and without even holding the rope, or looking at it, she climbed down like a monkey, seeming to find handholds and footholds by magic. The others watched her admiringly. Soon she was standing beside them. George was untying Timmy.

'Thanks awfully, Jo,' said George, looking up gratefully at Jo. 'You're a wonder. Tim must have been frightfully heavy.'

'He was,' said Jo, giving him a pat. 'I nearly dropped him. Well – what's the next move?'

'We'll hunt round this queer little cove a bit and see if there's any place we can hide,' said Julian. 'You go that way, George, and we'll go this.'

They parted, and began to hunt for a hiding-place. As far as Julian and Dick could see there was none at all, at least on the side they were exploring. The sea swept into the cove, swelling and subsiding – and just outside the great waves battered on to the rocks. There was certainly no chance of swimming out.

There was suddenly an excited shriek from George. 'JU! Come here. Look what I've found!'

They all rushed round to where George was standing, behind a big ledge of rock. She pointed to a great mass of something draped with seaweed.

'A boat! It's covered with seaweed – but it's a boat!'

'It's *your* boat!' yelled Dick, suddenly, and began to pull the fronds of seaweed madly off the hidden boat. 'Markhoff *didn't* smash it! It's here, perfectly all right. He couldn't find it – it was hidden so well with seaweed – so he just came back to Red and told him a lie.'

'He didn't smash it!' shouted Jo, and she, too, began to pull away the seaweed. 'It's quite all right – there's nothing wrong with it. He didn't smash it!'

The four children were so tremendously surprised and joyful that they thumped each other ridiculously on the back, and leapt about like mad things. They had their boat after all – George's good, sound boat. They could escape, hip hip hurrah!

A roar from above made them fall silent.

They gazed up, startled. Markhoff and the other two men were on the ledge far above, shouting and shaking their fists.

'You wait till we get you!' yelled Markhoff.

'Quick, quick!' said Julian, urgently, pulling at the boat. 'We've got just a chance. Pull her down to the water, pull hard!'

Markhoff was now coming down the cliff, and Jo wished she had untied the rope before she herself had climbed down, for Markhoff was finding it very useful. She tugged at the boat with the others, wishing it wasn't so heavy.

The boat was almost down to the water when something happened. Timmy, who had been gazing at everything in a most bewildered manner, suddenly slid off the

ledge he was on and fell straight into the sea. George gave
a scream.

'Oh, Timmy! He's in the water, quick, quick – he's
too doped to swim! He'll drown!'

Julian and Dick didn't dare to stop heaving at the
boat, because they could see that Markhoff would soon
be down beside them. George rushed to Timmy, who
was splashing around in the waves, still looking surprised
and bemused.

But the water had an amazing effect on him. It was
cold and it seemed to bring him to his senses quite suddenly. He became much more lively and swam strongly
to the rock off which he had slipped. He clambered out
with George's help, barking loudly.

The boat slid into the water, and Julian grabbed at
George. 'Come on. In you get. Buck up!'

Jo was in the boat and so was Dick. George, trying to
clutch at Timmy, was hauled in, too. Julian took a des-
pairing look at Markhoff, who was almost at the end
of the rope, about to jump down. They just wouldn't
get off in time!

Timmy suddenly slipped out of George's grasp and
tore madly over to the cliff barking warningly. He seemed
to be perfectly all right. The sudden coldness of the sea
had washed away all his dopeyness and sleepiness. Timmy
was himself again!

Markhoff was about five feet above the ledge when he
heard Timmy barking. He looked down in horror and
saw the big dog trying to jump up at him. He tried to
climb up quickly, out of Timmy's reach.

'Woof!' barked Timmy. 'Woof, woof, woof! Grrrrrrr!'

'Look out – he'll have your foot off!' yelled one of the men above on the ledge

'He's mad – angry – he's savage. Look out Mark!'

Markhoff *was* looking out! He was terrified. He clambered up another few feet, and then found that Timmy was making runs at the cliff to try and get up after him. He went up a bit further and clung to the rope with one hand, afraid of falling and being pounced on by the furious Timmy.

'Come on, Timmy!' suddenly cried George. 'Come on!'

The four of them had now got the boat on the waves, and if only they had Timmy they could set off and row round the rocks at the cave entrance before Markhoff could possibly reach them.

'Timmy! Timmy!'

Timmy heard, cast a last regretful look at Markhoff's legs, and bounded across to the boat. He leapt right in and stood there, still barking madly.

Markhoff dropped down the rope to the ledge – but he was too late. The boat shot out to the entrance of the cove and rounded it. In half a minute it had disappeared round the rocky corner and was out at sea.

Julian and Dick rowed steadily. George put her arms round Timmy and buried her face in his fur. Jo did the same.

'He's all right again, quite all right,' said George, happily.

'Yes, falling into the cold water did it,' agreed Jo, ruffling up his fur. 'Good old Timmy!'

Timmy was now snuffling about in the bottom of the boat joyfully. He had smelt a lovely smell. Jo wondered what he had found. Then she knew.

'It's the packet of sandwiches we brought with us in the boat and never ate!' she cried. 'Good old Timmy — he's wolfing the lot!'

'Let him!' said Julian, pulling hard at the oars. 'He deserves them all! My word, it's nice to hear his bark again and see his tail wagging.'

And wag it certainly did. It never stopped. The world had come right again for Timmy, he could see and hear properly again, he could bark and caper and jump — and he had his beloved George with him once more.

'Now for home,' said Julian. 'Anne *will* be pleased to see us. Gosh, what a time we've had!'

Chapter Twenty-Five

EVERYTHING OKAY

IT was getting dark as George's boat came into Kirrin Bay. It had seemed a very long pull indeed, and everyone was tired out. The girls had helped in the rowing when the boys had almost collapsed from exhaustion, and Timmy had cheered everyone up by his sudden high spirits.

'Honestly, his tail hasn't stopped wagging since he got into the boat,' said George. 'He's so pleased to be himself again!'

A small figure was on the beach as they came in, half-lost in the darkness. It was Anne. She called out to them in a trembling voice.

'Is it really you? I've been watching for you all day long! Are you all right?'

'Rather! And we've got George and Timmy, too!' shouted back Dick, as the boat scraped on the shingle. 'We're fine!'

They jumped out, Timmy too, and hauled the boat up the beach. Anne gave a hand, almost crying with joy to have them all again.

'It's bad enough being in the middle of an adventure,' she said, 'but it's much, much worse when you're left out. I'll never be left out again!'

'Woof,' said Timmy, wagging his tail in full agreement. He never wanted to be left out of adventures either!

They all went home – rather slowly, because they were so tired. Joan was on the look-out for them, as she had been all day. She screamed for joy when she saw George. 'George! You've got George at last! Oh, you bad children, you've been away all day and I didn't know where and I've been worried to death. George, are you all right?'

'Yes, thank you,' said George, who felt as if she was about to fall asleep at any moment. 'I just want something to eat before I fall absolutely sound asleep!'

'But where have you been all day? What have you been doing?' cried Joan, as she bustled off to get them a meal.

'I got so worked up I went to the police – and what a silly I felt – I couldn't tell them where you'd gone or anything. All I could say was you'd gone to find a man called Red, and had rowed away in George's boat!'

'The police have been up and down the coast in a motor-boat ever since,' said Anne. 'Trying to spot you, but they couldn't.'

'No. Our boat was well hidden,' said Dick. 'And so were we! So well hidden that I began to think we'd stay hidden for the rest of our lives.'

The telephone bell rang. Julian jumped. 'Oh, good – you've had the telephone mended. I'll go and 'phone the police when you've answered this call, Joan.'

But it was the police themselves on the telephone, very pleased to hear Joan saying excitedly that all the children were back safely. 'We'll be up in ten minutes,' they said.

In ten minutes' time the five children and Timmy were tucking into a good meal. 'Don't stop,' said the police sergeant, when he came into the room with the constable the children had seen before. 'Just talk while you're eating.'

So they talked. They told about every single thing. First George told a bit, then Jo, then Dick then Julian. At first the sergeant was bewildered, but then the bits of information began to piece themselves together in his mind like a jigsaw puzzle.

'Will my father go to prison?' asked Jo.

'I'm afraid so,' said the sergeant.

'Bad luck, Jo,' said Dick.

'I don't mind,' said Jo. 'I'm better off when he's away — I don't have to do things he tells me then.'

'We'll see if we can't fix you up with a nice home,' said the sergeant kindly. 'You've run wild, Jo — you want looking after.'

'I don't want to go to a Home for Bad Girls,' said Jo, looking scared.

'I shan't let you,' said Dick. 'You're one of the pluckiest kids I've ever known. We'll none of us let you go to a Home. We'll find someone who'll be kind to you someone like — like . . .'

'Like *me*,' said Joan, who was listening, and she put her arm rouund Jo and gave her a squeeze. 'I've got a cousin who'd like a ragamuffin like you – a bad little girl with a very good heart. Don't you fret. We'll look after you.'

'I wouldn't mind living with somebody like you,' said Jo, in an offhand way. 'I wouldn't be mean any more then, and I daresay I wouldn't be bad. I'd like to see Dick and all of you sometimes, though.'

'You will if you're good,' said Dick, with a grin. 'But mind – if I ever hear you've got in at anyone's pantry window again, or anything like that, I'll never see you again!'

Jo grinned. She was very happy. She suddenly remembered something and put her hand into the little rush basket she still carried. She took out an enormous key.

'Here you are,' she said to the sergeant. 'Here's the key to the tower room. I bet Red and the others are still locked up there, ready for you to catch! My, won't they get a shock when *you* unlock the door and walk in!'

'Quite a lot of people are going to get shocks,' said the sergeant, putting away his very full note-book. 'Miss Georgina, you're lucky to get away unharmed, you and your dog. By the way, we got in touch with a friend of your father's, when we tried to find out about those papers that were stolen. He says your father gave him all his important American papers before he went – so this fellow Red hasn't anything of value at all. He went to all his trouble for nothing.'

'Do you know anything about Red?' asked Julian. 'He seemed a bit mad to me.'

'If he's the fellow we think he is, he's not very sane,'

said the sergeant. 'We'll be glad to have him under lock and key – and that man Markhoff too. He's not as clever as Red, but he's dangerous.'

'I hope he hasn't escaped in that helicopter,' said Dick. 'He meant to go tonight.'

'Well, we'll be there in under an hour or so,' said the sergeant. 'I'll just use your telephone, if I may, and set things going '

Things were certainly set going that night! Cars roared up to Red's house, and the gate was broken in when no one came to open it. The helicopter was still in the yard – but alas! it was on its side, smashed beyond repair. The children were told afterwards that Markhoff and the other two men had tried to set off in it, but there was something wrong – and it had risen some way and then fallen back to the yard.

The old woman was trying to look after the three hurt men, who had crawled from their seats and gone to bathe their cuts and bruises. Markhoff had hurt his head, and showed no fight at all.

'And what about Red?' the sergeant asked Markhoff. 'Is he still locked up?'

'Yes,' said Markhoff, savagely. 'And a good thing, too. You'll have to break that door down with a battering-ram to get him and the others out.'

'Oh no, we shan't,' said the sergeant, and produced the key. Markhoff stared at it.

'That kid!' he said. 'She gave me the key of the larder. Wait till I get her – she'll be sorry.'

'It'll be a long wait, Markhoff,' said the sergeant. 'A

long, long wait. We'll have to take you off with us, I'm afraid.'

Red, Simmy and Jake were still locked up, and were mad with rage. But they saw that the game was up, and it wasn't long before all of them were safely tucked away in police cars.

'A very, very nice little haul,' said the sergeant to one of his men. 'Very neat, too – three of them all locked up ready for us!'

'What about that kid, Jo?' said the man. 'She seems a bad lot, and as clever as they make them!'

'She's going to have a chance now,' said the sergeant. 'Everybody has a chance sometimes, and this is hers. She's just about half-and-half. I reckon – half bad and half good. But she'll be all right now she's got a chance!'

Jo was sleeping in Joan's room again. The rest were in their own bedrooms, getting ready for bed. They suddenly didn't feel sleepy any more. Timmy especially was very lively, darting in and out of the rooms, and sending the landing mats sliding about all over the place.

'Timmy! If you jump on my bed again I'll slam the door on you!' threatened Anne. But she didn't, of course. It was so lovely to see old Timmy quite himself once more.

The telephone bell suddenly rang, and made everyone jump.

'*Now* what's up?' said Julian, and went down in the hall to answer it. A voice spoke in his ear.

'Is that Kirrin 011? This is Telegrams. There is a cable for you, with reply prepaid. I am now going to read it.'

'Go ahead,' said Julian.

'It is from Seville in Spain,' said the voice, 'and reads as follows:

"HERE IS OUR ADDRESS. PLEASE CABLE BACK SAY-
ING IF EVERYTHING ALL RIGHT — UNCLE QUENTIN".'

Julian repeated the message to the others, who had now crowded round him in the hall. 'What reply shall I give?' he asked. 'No good upsetting them now everything is over!'

'Not a bit of good,' said Dick. 'Say what you like!'

'Right!' said Julian, and turned to the telephone again. 'Hallo — here is the reply message, please. Ready?

"HAVING A MOST EXCITING TIME, WITH LOTS OF FUN
AND GAMES. EVERYTHING OKAY — JULIAN".'

'Everything okay,' repeated Anne, as they went up-stairs to bed once more 'That's what I like to hear at the end of an adventure. Everything okay.'

A complete list of the FAMOUS FIVE ADVENTURES by Enid Blyton

If any of these is not available in a Knight paperback edition, it can be bought in a hard-cover edition published by Brockhampton Press.

These are other Knight Books

THE HERON RIDE
Mary Treadgold

On a warm, summer evening, at sundown,
Sandra and her brother Adam stood in a
cottage garden, watching a line of riders
cantering across the skyline of the Downs.
Sandra – for whom life had been tough
and sad – longed to be riding with them.
But for her there was no horse, and there
was no money.
This is the story of how she and Adam
became so involved in the fortunes of these
six riders that, in the end, her luck turned.

BAMBI
Felix Salten

The original story of Bambi, the forest deer,
from his first unsteady steps as a fawn to
the time when he becomes a proud and
majestic stag, a creature of infinite grace
and beauty, all powerful, and wise in
forest lore.
Newly illustrated by Maurice Wilson, the
famous artist whose drawings and paintings
of nature are widely known.